W9-BRE-208

ROBBER'S TRAIL

ROBBER'S TRAIL

W. W. Lee

Walker and Company
New York

All the characters and events portrayed in this work are fictitious.

First published in the United States of America in 1992
by Walker Publishing Company, Inc.

Published simultaneously in Canada by Thomas Allen & Son
Canada, Limited, Markham, Ontario

Library of Congress Cataloging-in-Publication Data
Lee, W. W. (Wendi W.)
Robber's trail / W. W. Lee.
p.   cm.
ISBN 0-8027-4133-9 (cloth)
I. Title.
PS3562.E3663R63   1992
813'.54—dc20   92-5242
CIP

Printed in the United States of America

2 4 6 8 10 9 7 5 3 1

For Ed Gorman,
friend and mentor

CHAPTER 1

MARSHAL Tyrell McManus was whittling, propped in a chair in front of his office on a slow, hot afternoon in Nevada City when he heard the sudden, sharp sound of a gunshot from the other end of town. Out on the street, people froze momentarily, then women began pulling their young children out of harm's way and men scattered, some automatically drawing their guns or running inside their stores for a shotgun.

Earl Dunlap, the assay clerk, stepped outside to see what was going on; was the first to notice the small figure scurrying toward them. "It's Cyrus Dundee," he shouted at Marshal McManus, then pointed down the street. McManus jammed his hat farther down on his head, patted his gun reassuringly, and strode toward the figure. Dundee's arms were flapping awkwardly in the air, as if he were a large bird trying to fly. The sun was winking off of his bifocals. Marshal McManus quickened his pace.

"The bank's been robbed! Joe's been shot," Dundee cried out in a high-pitched voice, his face red, drops of sweat on his balding brow. McManus grabbed Dundee by the elbows to steady him.

"Slow down, Cyrus," he said. "Joe's been shot?" He turned to Jim Wells, his chubby, baby-faced deputy, and said, "Get the doctor, Jim. Then get a posse together as fast as you can. Meet us at the bank at the south end of town."

As his deputy mounted his horse and rode off at a gallop toward the doctor's surgery, the marshal turned

1

back to Cyrus and asked, "Was anyone else hurt? Who was in the bank when it happened?"

"Nobody else was there. Mr. Rhodes went home for lunch an hour ago. Business was slow, so I went to the diner for a while. When I got back I found Joe . . ."

"Who did it?" McManus asked.

Cyrus was shaking, almost crying, but with effort, he managed to talk as they hurried toward the bank. "It was a gang, Marshal," he said. "They took off on their horses."

"Which way?"

Cyrus became anxious. He said the gang left town headed south. Probably southwest, out of California toward Nevada Territory.

"How many?" McManus asked.

The bank clerk had taken off his bifocals and was mopping the sweat from his brow with a linen handkerchief. "I don't know, Marshal. Four, maybe five. They were leaving through the front door just as I was coming back from my lunch. I always come in the side door."

McManus felt a twinge of disappointment that Cyrus had not got a good look at the outlaws. But he might still be able to describe their clothes and maybe their horses.

Doc Holder, a tall, thin man nearing fifty years old, pulled up in his horse and buggy as McManus and Cyrus reached the front of the bank. He clambered down and hurried toward them, his black bag dangling from his left hand.

"Jim came running into my office," Doc said, his face flushed with excitement. "He told me someone shot Joe Child."

"The bank was robbed," McManus explained. "Come on." The marshal drew his gun, as a precaution, and led the way into the bank.

The Nevada City Bank was a small neat wooden building with a large front window and mahogany doors. The bank owner, Vernon Rhodes, had once told Tyrell McManus that he'd had the doors shipped out from the East Coast specially for his building. He wanted the place to have a little class when it opened for business three years ago.

It was deathly quiet inside the bank. The faint smell of gunpowder hung in the air. There was no sign of Joe Child in the front half of the bank.

The marshal and Doc Holder followed Cyrus Dundee through a half-door to the right of the teller windows. McManus shuddered at the sight that greeted them. Joe Child was sprawled facedown on the floor, in a pool of blood. From what McManus could see, he had been shot in the side near the heart. He doubted there was anything Doc could do.

But Doc Holder went through all the motions. He knelt beside Joe and lifted his wrist, feeling for a pulse. He put his ear to the victim's chest to listen for a heartbeat. Finally, he took out a small mirror and held it under the victim's nose, waiting for a sign of life. Finally, he put the mirror away, straightened up, and, shaking his head slowly, said, "He's dead, Ty. Someone's going to have to tell Kathleen."

Marshal McManus didn't know what to say, so he remained silent. Cyrus was fidgeting beside him, taking his bifocals off and dabbing at his face again with his handkerchief.

Jim came into the bank to give a report. "Some of the men are getting their horses ready now. I told them to meet us here in a few minutes."

"Good, Jim. You'll have to deputize them and start without me, though. I'll look over things here at the bank first," McManus said. "I'll ride after you later. Get someone to run over to tell Vernon Rhodes that his bank was just robbed."

Jim nodded his understanding and ran out of the bank.

The doctor followed, saying, "I'll be back with a couple of men to move the body."

McManus regretted having to give this awful news to Joe's wife. But for the moment he pushed the unpleasant thought out of his mind and turned to the task of looking for any identifying sign that the gang might have left behind.

It looked like a straightforward robbery. The safe was wide open and empty. The teller drawers had been yanked open and cleaned out as well.

"How much money was taken, Cyrus?" McManus asked.

The bank clerk kept pushing nervously at his bifocals, beads of sweat on his brow. "Well, you see, Marshal," he replied, "there was almost three hundred dollars in deposits here until yesterday when Wells Fargo came into town and dropped off the railroad payroll. It was going to be picked up later today. There was close to one thousand dollars in payroll alone."

"Over a thousand," McManus muttered. He felt his heart sinking. He'd forgotten. Yesterday, he'd ridden a few miles out of town to meet the Wells Fargo stagecoach, which was carrying the railroad payroll. He had personally accompanied the payroll to the bank. "How'd the robbers get into the safe?"

Cyrus Dundee shook his head, a frown appearing on his face. "I don't rightly know, Marshal. Like I said, I was walking back to the bank after my noon meal when I heard a shot fired. When I came into the bank through the side door, I found Joe lying on the floor. He was already too far gone, so I ran to the front door and looked out. I barely got a look at the robbers before they mounted their horses and headed out of town."

The short, portly, well-dressed banker burst into the bank. Vernon Rhodes was puffing hard and red-faced, as if he'd been running, which he probably had been doing. "I just heard what happened," he said, looking around. He gave the teller's body a brief glance before his gaze rested on the open safe. "Where's the payroll?" he asked in a panic-stricken voice as he looked around in vain for the money.

"Mr. Rhodes," Cyrus said nervously, and unnecessarily, "we've been robbed. Joe is dead!"

Vernon Rhodes gave a withering glance to his bank clerk and snapped, "I can see that for myself, Dundee. But how did that safe get opened?"

McManus was annoyed. He'd never cared much for Vernon Rhodes, and his appalling behavior made McManus dislike the bank owner even more. It was understandable that he would be distressed about the money, but he showed total disregard for the death of his employee.

The marshal kept his feelings about Rhodes to himself and asked, "How many people had access to the safe's combination, Mr. Rhodes?"

"Just myself and Cyrus," he replied, turning and glaring at the clerk. "You must have been here during the robbery. You must have opened the safe for them."

Cyrus shook his head and cringed. "No, no," the bank clerk replied, his voice high with fear. "I tell you, I was just coming back from my lunch and this is what I found." He turned for appeal to the marshal. "Joe didn't have the safe combination, but he knew where Mr. Rhodes kept the numbers—he'd seen Mr. Rhodes consulting the slip of paper in his desk drawer often enough."

McManus gave a querying look at the banker.

Vernon Rhodes grunted, a sheepish expression on his face. "Well, I might have to refresh my memory occasionally," he conceded, "but I never thought anyone ever noticed." He rubbed his face and looked around, a moan escaping. "How am I ever going to recover from this? What are the depositors going to say?"

Suddenly there was a ruckus at the bank door. Wilmer Colbert, publisher of the *Nevada City Gazette*, came inside. Marshal McManus watched the tall, loose-jointed man and thought that Colbert looked like a marionette that had been carelessly put together.

"I hear Joe Child was killed in a bank robbery, Marshal," Colbert began. "How much did the bank robbers get away with? Did anyone see them?"

"I don't want this man in my bank, Marshal," Rhodes said in a fierce tone. "Get him out of here."

Wilmer Colbert flashed a quick sardonic smile in Rhodes's direction. It seemed he didn't like Rhodes any more than McManus did. "I don't think you have any say over what I do or don't print, Mr. Rhodes. This is front-page news."

Cyrus Dundee stepped forward and meekly said, "I saw them leaving. I came in here right after I heard the shot."

Wilmer Colbert grinned grimly at the clerk and moved over to him. "Maybe I can ask you a few questions, Cyrus."

"Marshal!" Rhodes barked.

McManus stepped in the middle and raised a conciliatory hand. "Now, Mr. Rhodes. Wilmer Colbert has a right to be here. I'm not happy about it either, but it's one of the freedoms we enjoy."

Colbert's grin turned nasty as he looked at Rhodes. "It's called freedom of the press, Vernon," he said. With a flourish, he took out a pencil and pad of paper and looked at the bank clerk. "Tell me, Cyrus, when did this happen?"

Eyes wide, Cyrus Dundee straightened up. "Really? You want to interview me and it'll be on the front page?"

Vernon Rhodes's face turned beet red and he started wheezing. "Now just a doggone minute here. You can't come in here and interview my employee without my permission."

Cyrus Dundee shrank back. It was well known that Rhodes and Colbert didn't get along. Rhodes liked to put on airs, and Colbert enjoyed baiting the bank owner. On occasion, he'd been known to take Rhodes down a peg or two with a well-chosen word.

McManus had just about had enough. He had come to the bank in an effort to investigate and instead was being called on for diplomacy. He took charge of the situation by addressing Vernon Rhodes. "Mr. Rhodes, I think you might be better off going home for now. Cyrus here will lock up when everything's done." The grumbling bank owner reluctantly left his bank. Then the marshal turned to Colbert and said, "Maybe you can get Dundee's story later."

Wilmer Colbert scowled. "You're interfering with the right of the people to know, Marshal."

McManus smiled. "Right now, you're interfering with me getting my job done. You're welcome to stop by my office later tonight and I'll give you whatever I know."

Grudgingly, Colbert left, and the marshal returned to the business at hand. It had been over ten minutes since they had entered the bank and he hadn't heard the posse passing by. The trail was growing colder by the minute. McManus knew from long experience that they had already lost any advantage, and apprehending the bank robbers would now be just a case of plain dumb luck.

His thoughts were interrupted by the sound of a buggy pulling up outside. Two scruffy-looking men entered the bank and warily looked around. From his position behind the teller's cage, McManus recognized the men as Rollins and Cutter, former miners who had sold their stake when the land had been played out; they now did odd jobs around town and drank up most of their profits. McManus had occasionally had the pleasure of their company in jail whenever they got a little too drunk and rowdy.

With a sheet draped over his right arm, Cutter stepped forward and touched his cap, calling out, "Afternoon, Marshal. We're here workin' for Mr. Gould." Henry Gould was the town undertaker. Once in a while, he hired Rollins and Cutter for grave digging and transporting bodies.

The marshal signaled them to come to the back of the

bank and they complied. But they still hung back, eyeing the body. McManus urged them on, saying, "Go ahead, boys. Joe's not going to get up and *walk* down to Gould's place."

As they bent over their task, Rollins began to look a little green around the gills, but he followed Cutter's lead. They wrapped the body up in the sheet, then hoisted Joe Child between them. McManus held open the door between the teller's cage and the front of the bank as Rollins and Cutter maneuvered the body out onto the wagon.

McManus heard the faint staccato of horses' hooves coming this way. Jim must have finally gotten the posse together, he thought. He turned to Cyrus and said, "I'm joining the posse after I ride out to see Joe's widow. But when I get back, I'll want you to come over to my office and go through your story once more."

"But I told you . . . ," the clerk began.

McManus frowned and said sternly, "You may remember something later on. Now go home and rest up. I may be calling on you later tonight." He turned and left.

CHAPTER 2

JOE Child's house was located on the far edge of town. It was doubtful that his wife had heard the commotion earlier in the day, unless she had been shopping at the general store. Since she hadn't come down to the bank, McManus reasoned, she must not have heard about the robbery.

It was a small house that had been made pretty and pleasant by Kathleen's work. She had planted wildflowers in the front, and a low picket fence ran around the place. McManus and his wife had known the Childs for five years, ever since McManus came to Nevada City to take the marshal's job.

Kathleen Child opened the door. "I saw you coming from down the street," she called. "How are you, Ty? Joe is still at work and I'm about to start making dinner."

McManus took off his hat, a solemn look on his face. "Kathleen, I haven't come here with good news. There was a robbery at the bank today."

She became very still, worry showing on her face. "Robbery, you say? Joe was working . . ." She trailed off, her face turning white as it slowly dawned on her. The marshal's grave expression and his silence were enough. "No," she whispered. "Joe's not hurt, is he?"

At that moment, McManus hated his job more than anything. He tried to say it gently, but he knew there was no way to soften the blow. "Kathleen, Joe was killed."

She slumped against the door frame. He thought for a moment that she might faint.

9

In a faltering voice, she asked, "What happened? Did you catch the man who did it?"

McManus looked away. His fingers began worrying the brim of his hat. "They haven't been caught yet. I suspect it was the Shirley gang that's been robbing a lot of banks nearby. We put a posse together." He shook his head. "I'm still investigating. Cyrus Dundee came in after Joe was shot. He may have some information that could identify them."

Her face was buried in her hands by now, her shoulders gently shaking.

"I'm sorry. Kathleen. I'm doing the best I can. I'll do everything in my power to get the—" McManus stopped himself from saying "son-of-a-bitch" in front of the new widow. He searched for an adequate substitute, ending with, "the man who did this."

She took a few deep breaths, then dropped her hands to her sides. Since the news of her husband's death, she looked suddenly older. McManus felt guilty.

"I know you'll do your best, Marshal. I have to see him. Is Joe at Henry Gould's undertaking parlor?"

He nodded. "Do you want me to go with you?"

She managed a bleak smile. "No, Marshal. Thank you for coming by to give me the news, but I won't keep you. You find the men who did this to Joe."

"If there's anything I can do, that Lottie can do . . ."

"Thank you. I'll let you or your wife know." She stepped back inside and closed the door softly.

McManus caught up to the posse just before they reached the Potter house, which was considered the Nevada City limit. Deputy Wells was at the front of the group of men, scanning the horizon, a puzzled look on his face. "This trail is used so heavily that it's hard to tell which way the gang went," he explained.

McManus followed Wells's gaze. There was a clear trail

that was often used. Wagon ruts and horses' hooves had trampled the earth, and unless a man was an expert in tracking, it was difficult to determine whether the last horse passed this way hours or only minutes ago. Unfortunately, no one in the posse had that experience. Besides, if the Shirley gang was as wily as the poster led him to believe, they wouldn't necessarily leave any sign.

On the marshal's orders, the posse split up into three groups and fanned out in several different directions, weaving in and out of the mazelike hills, hoping to pick up some fresh tracks. But after two hours, most of the men had given up.

Finally, Marshal McManus drew his revolver and fired three shots into the air, a signal that had been agreed upon by the posse to mean that the pursuit was at an end. The sun had gone down by the time the discouraged and bedraggled men reached the outskirts of Nevada City. Tyrell McManus turned to the group and said, "You all did as much as can be asked of any man. Thanks for your help. Now go on home to your wives and dinners."

Cal Stokes, a large youth with a crooked nose, spoke up. "What are you going to do now, Marshal?"

Most of the men nodded in assent, worried looks on their faces. McManus was well aware that a couple of the men in the posse were on the railroad company's payroll. They were concerned about going without their wages from the stolen payroll.

The marshal sighed heavily and replied, "I still have several leads to follow. Go on home, men, and we'll talk in the morning." He turned to his deputy and added, "You, too, Jim. I'm going back to the office to get some work done."

Jim nodded and said, "I may come by after dinner, Ty. I don't know if I could get much sleep after today's excitement."

McManus had a thought. "Cyrus's house is on your way

home. Could you let him know that I want to talk to him now? He can meet me at my office in about half an hour."

"He'll be there," Jim promised. With that, the deputy touched his hat and rode off in the direction of his home. As if Jim's departure was the catalyst, the rest of the posse broke up, heading off in various directions.

On his way back to the office, Marshal McManus mulled over the events of the day. This had been the first bank robbery Nevada City had ever seen, and chances were that if the gang got away with it once, they would think they could get away with it again. He would have to put the next payroll under heavy guard—he'd have to convince Vernon Rhodes to hire armed guards at the bank for the time that the payroll was in the bank safe. Knowing how tight Rhodes could be with a dollar, McManus wasn't so sure the bank owner would like the idea of parting with money so easily, even if it meant saving money in the long run.

But that was a long-term plan. He still had to have another talk with Cyrus Dundee. Maybe the clerk could provide more information that could lead to the identification of the bank robbers.

When he got back to the office, McManus lit his desk lantern. A covered tray was sitting on his desk, and when he pulled back the cloth, the fragrant aroma of buffalo meat stew and dumplings wafted past him. A small pail of foamy beer accompanied his meal. His stomach growled loudly, and it was then that he realized that he hadn't eaten since that morning. Thank goodness his wife, Lottie, took care of such necessities for him.

McManus sat down and tucked the cloth into his dusty cotton shirt. As he poised his spoon over the stew, a thought came to him and he dropped it as quick as he'd picked it up. He pushed his meal away, pulled open a protesting desk drawer full of wanted posters, and shuffled through them, pausing to read an occasional one.

Dreary thoughts of what had happened that afternoon kept running through his head.

A frown creased his forehead when he got to a torn and wrinkled poster announcing a one-hundred-dollar reward for the capture of the Shirley gang. He peered at the words in the dim lamplight, then took out his magnifying glass to enlarge the descriptions. Fergis, Vardis, Homer, and Clyde Shirley were four brothers from the Kentucky hills who migrated to California at the end of the Gold Rush.

"Last seen in Grass Valley, California," the poster read. "Robbed the Grass Valley Bank." Grass Valley was darn close to Nevada City. The marshal shifted in his chair. He didn't want to jump to any conclusions, but it was a good possibility that the Shirleys could be the gang that robbed the bank this afternoon. They were known to leave town, disappear into the hills, and split up, which was a quick way of losing a posse.

There was a timid knock on the door. Cyrus Dundee came in and walked over to the marshal's desk, the glow of the kerosene lamp reflecting in his bifocals.

"Thanks for coming down, Cyrus," McManus said.

"I'm still a little shaken by what happened, Marshal," the bank clerk said, looking rattled by the fact that he'd escaped death this afternoon by a few seconds.

The marshal handed over the pile of wanted posters to Dundee. "Here you go, Cyrus. See if you can pick out your bank robbers from this." He sat back and ate his dinner while the bank clerk slowly studied each poster. It was going to be a long night.

A few days after the robbery, Vernon Rhodes strode into Marshal McManus's office. The bank owner looked a little brighter than the last time McManus had seen him. "Must be good news, Mr. Rhodes. Have the outlaws been captured?"

McManus hadn't been able to concentrate all his attention on the robbery and murder. He'd had to settle a land
dispute between a farmer and a rancher whose land bor-
dered the farmer's orchard. The rancher's cattle had been
wandering over onto the farmer's property and had trampled several sapling fruit trees. Shots were exchanged, and
McManus had been sent out to calm down both parties.

"No, Marshal, I just thought you should know that I've
talked to Harold Valentine, the owner of the Grass Valley
Bank."

"Wasn't that bank robbed about a month ago?"

"Yes, yes, by the same gang that robbed my bank,"
Vernon Rhodes replied, practically beaming with pleasure.
McManus wondered what he was so pleased about and he
soon found out. "We've taken the liberty of hiring someone to investigate."

The marshal raised his eyebrows. "What kind of someone?"

"Not a gunslinger, I assure you," Rhodes said hastily. "A
man named Jefferson Birch. He works for an agency that
specializes in investigations of this sort."

"Where is this agency located?" McManus asked with
suspicion. He didn't trust anyone who wasn't a lawman.

"San Francisco. Mr. Valentine has vouched for them. His
brother, Gerald, lives there and looked up the agency. Mr.
Birch works for an outfit that calls itself Tisdale Investigations. Gerald Valentine visited the office in our behalf and
explained the situation to the owner of the agency. Mr.
Birch was recommended for the job." He pulled out some
papers and added, "Mr. Birch will be arriving tomorrow."

"Is he some kind of bounty hunter?"

"No, he's not," Rhodes assured him before handing over
one of the papers to the marshal, adding, "Here are his
qualifications. I expect you will cooperate, Marshal." With
that, he left.

McManus read over the paper and, in spite of himself,

found Jefferson Birch's record to be impressive. He had been a Texas Ranger for five years, then traveled farther west, doing odd jobs between assignments for Tisdale. He had caught a gang of road agents who worked out of Grant's Pass in Oregon, which McManus remembered hearing about from another marshal passing through Nevada City. Birch had also worked on a case in Nevada, tracking down an alleged killer, then proving someone else committed the crime.

The way this Birch fellow's record read, he must solve a new case every day before lunch, McManus thought wryly. The marshal wasn't sure how he felt about some flamboyant stranger coming into town and taking over. Of course, it was Vernon Rhodes's bank, and certainly it was his choice to hire this man, sight unseen. Maybe Birch's record was as good as it looked on paper, or maybe Rhodes and Valentine were just being handed a lot of manure.

Marshal McManus looked down at the letter that had been prepared for him by a fellow named Arthur Tisdale.

Dear Marshal McManus,

This is to inform you that my agent, Jefferson Birch, has been retained to investigate the possible connection between the robberies that took place at the Grass Valley Bank and the Nevada City Bank. This is to assure you that Mr. Birch will fully cooperate with you and I trust that you will do the same. He will need to be informed of what has transpired so he can coordinate the information on the robberies of both banks.

Mr. Birch will be arriving soon after you receive this letter. If there is any need to get in touch with me for any reason, please do not hesitate. I remain,

Yours Truly,
Arthur Tisdale.

The marshal reread the letter slowly, his eyes narrowing slightly. Who did this Tisdale fellow think Jefferson Birch was, the king of England? He was just going to waltz in here and take over the investigation.

Ever since the robbery, McManus had felt the resentment of the townsfolk, real or imagined. He had to be fair: no one had actually said anything to him. If people did harbor a grudge against him, he really couldn't blame them. A lot of townsfolk had lost their savings in the robbery, and they had been counting on their marshal to recover it. And he felt as if he had failed them.

In his mind, he ticked off what hadn't been done: he hadn't gotten the posse together fast enough. He hadn't picked up the trail in the hills. And he hadn't saved Joe Child. That was worst of all. There was no reason for him to assume there was trouble at the bank until Dundee came down the street, but maybe, after hearing the shot, he should have jumped right on his horse and checked the bank, just to be sure. He didn't know anything about doctoring, but maybe if he had been there right away, he could have done something for Joe.

He recalled the funeral, which had taken place the day after the robbery. All of Nevada City had attended the service up on Great Beyond Hill, even society-conscious Vernon Rhodes and his wife. After Joe had been laid to rest, McManus and his wife had extended their condolences to Kathleen. As they turned to leave, the widow grabbed McManus's arm, her eyes so intense that they seemed as if they could burn a hole through the black netting of her mourning hat. "Have you found the man who killed my Joe yet, Marshal?"

A hush fell over the crowd of people who were waiting to console Kathleen Child. He didn't know what to say. There had been very little progress.

"Cyrus Dundee identified the gang from a wanted poster, Kathleen," he finally had managed to say. "It's just a matter of time before the law catches up with them." It was as good as admitting that he wasn't going to be the one to find them. But it was the truth. She dropped her grip on his arm and nodded in resignation.

Now McManus rubbed his eyes and put down the letter of introduction from Tisdale Investigations. He should welcome the help of this Jefferson Birch, but McManus still felt reluctant about turning the facts over to this man who, although not just an ordinary citizen, was not quite the law.

CHAPTER 3

THE ride up north had been long and hot for Jefferson Birch. He slowed his horse, Cactus, down to a walk as the town of Grass Valley came into view. Birch took off his black hat and brushed it against his knee. Road dust flew off the brim and crest, making him sneeze and his eyes tear up. For the last three months, Birch had been working as a wrangler at a large horse ranch near Modesto. Every morning, he had woken up with aching muscles and creaking joints from busting broncs and rounding up mavericks. There were times he had come close to breaking a few bones as well.

The wire from Tisdale had come through just after the big rodeo in Modesto. Birch's boss had entered several of his ranch hands, including Birch, in the saddle bronc-riding event. Birch did well, but a wrangler from a rival ranch had come in with a better time.

The former Texas Ranger had been happy enough just to be able to walk away instead of being carried away like some of the other fellows. He knew that he was getting too old for horse busting. He preferred working on a cattle ranch where it was easier to guess what a steer would do.

It was a relief to be contacted by his sometime employer, Arthur Tisdale. Although investigation work didn't last as long as work on a cattle ranch, and there was more danger, the pay was better. Tisdale's wire had given him the name of the client he was to contact in Grass Valley.

Birch reached the edge of the town and dismounted, leading Cactus up the main street. Grass Valley was smaller than Modesto, but bigger than most of the podunk mining towns Birch had passed through on his way north. As he neared the center of town, the traffic began to grow heavy. Supply wagons, buggies, and several stagecoaches vied for space on the street as young boys and girls darted back and forth across the avenue.

Birch skirted the street and searched for the sheriff's office. A ten-year-old boy, intent on keeping his hoop going, brushed by Birch. The hoop began to wobble, then fell in the road.

"Excuse me, mister," the boy said as he righted his hoop.

"Where's the sheriff's office?" Birch asked.

The boy slowed down long enough to point to the other side of the street. "Farther down that way," he replied before jogging off alongside his steel hoop.

A smile tugged at one side of Birch's mouth as he watched the boy elbow his way past some friends. When the rowdy boys finally disappeared from view, Birch began looking for the sheriff's office. It was a modest building made of weathered gray wood with a small window to the right of the door. One of the glass panes had been broken and was patched over with a plank nailed on the outside. After hitching Cactus to a post outside, he entered the office.

A balding man wearing a sheriff's badge on his coat was perched behind a desk, writing up a report. His size overpowered the entire office, making it look like a child's room. Birch took off his dusty black hat. The sheriff looked up.

"What can I do for you, stranger?" the sheriff asked.

"My name is Jefferson Birch. You should have a letter of introduction here."

The sheriff pointed his pencil at Birch and asked, "You the man who's been hired to look into the bank robberies?"

Birch nodded. "I was hired by a Mr. Harold Valentine."

"Yup. He owns the Grass Valley Bank." The sheriff put down his pencil and started to sort through a pile of papers. "My name's Chester Martin, but you can call me Chet. I got that letter here somewhere." He pulled a piece of paper from the heap and peered at it. "Ah. Here it is. Now, let's see." He scanned the letter silently, then looked back up at Birch and said, "So you were a Ranger back in Texas."

"That was a few years ago," Birch admitted. He tried not to think much about the past.

"You're welcome to gather information, ask questions, whatever." Sheriff Martin put the letter down and leaned back, his chair tipping dangerously on two legs.

"I don't want to step on any toes," Birch said. He still wasn't sure what the sheriff's opinion was of the bank owner's decision to bring in a stranger on an ongoing investigation.

Martin shrugged. "Don't concern me none. It's a real good idea, come to think of it. You actually have two clients, Harold Valentine and the owner of the Nevada City Bank, Vernon Rhodes. I'm sure that when you meet with Mr. Valentine, he'll give you the necessary information. Although both banks were robbed, Marshal McManus and me haven't compared robberies. We've never gotten along too well as it is." He righted his chair and dug into the middle drawer, then handed Birch a cheap tin star. "You might as well be sworn in so's if you end up catching the culprits, you can bring them in right."

Birch reluctantly took the badge and repeated the standard oath given to deputized citizens. As Birch pinned the star on his black vest, the sheriff said, "So I suppose you need to be told as much as I know."

"That would help," Birch said, "but right now I know that I haven't eaten since this morning. Can you tell me where to find a good meal?"

The sheriff blinked in surprise, then grinned sheepishly. "I should have thought of that." He stood up, his chair groaning, as if in relief. Grabbing his hat from a coat rack, he said, "I haven't eaten either. Let's go down to Molly's."

Molly's looked like a saloon on the outside. The sign hanging above the door was painted in bright red and blue. On the sign next to Molly's name was a picture of a rooster hoisting a mug of beer. Birch stared at it in quiet amusement.

The inside also looked like a saloon. Birch was about to tell Sheriff Martin that he didn't want to drink his lunch, he needed something more substantial, when a short, squat woman with leathery skin and salt-and-pepper hair came up to them and, in a gruff voice, asked, "What'll it be, Chet?"

"Food, Molly." He indicated Birch and added, "This stranger just arrived and needs a good hot meal."

Molly put her hands on her ample hips and eyed Birch critically, finally proclaiming in a loud voice, "Looks like he needs a few good hot meals."

Several of the patrons roared their approval. Birch grinned and replied, "I'm sure you're just the one who can provide them."

Molly broke into a whoop of laughter, pounding Birch hard on the back. "You're all right, stranger. Come sit yourself down in the back here." She turned to Martin, who was still standing by the door, and asked, "You here to eat or gawk?"

They sat in a small room at the back that was apparently used by customers who wanted a meal with their drink. There was a long planklike table that someone had attempted to make more cheerful by covering with a stained white cotton tablecloth. A large mason jar filled with wilting daisies had been added as an afterthought. Birch and Sheriff Martin each took a seat. Both men took off their hats and placed them on the table. Molly seemed to appear out of nowhere, delivering two glasses of whiskey.

"I'll be right out with your grub," she said, then disappeared through the saloon door.

Birch turned to Martin and raised his eyebrows. The sheriff grinned in return and said, "You don't get a choice here at Molly's. You eat what she serves, but it's the best meal in town. Now, let's talk about what you're here to do. What do you know already?"

"Two banks have been robbed, one bank clerk killed in the process."

"The man that was killed was a teller at the Nevada City Bank. I have a list of names of the witnesses at the Grass Valley Bank robbery. When you're done here, you'll want to go to Nevada City and talk to the marshal there. It's no more than ten miles away."

"I'll also want to talk to the bank owners to get an idea of what they expect from me."

Sheriff Martin nodded.

Birch paused, then asked, "Do you have any idea who robbed the banks?"

"None of the witnesses here in Grass Valley can agree on which gang robbed them, but we've always suspected it was the Shirley gang. The witness over in Nevada City positively identified the Shirleys as robbing that bank and killing the teller." The sheriff frowned as he talked about the Shirleys.

Birch noticed and said, "Is something wrong, Sheriff? Maybe something that you don't agree with?"

Sheriff Martin shook his head, as if he were shaking off a troubling thought. He rubbed the back of his neck and replied, "It all fits, I suppose. I've read the wanted posters on these outlaws. They've been in this area for the last six months, robbing banks in Sacramento and smaller towns, so the fact that they robbed this bank would fit. But"—the lawman hesitated, then continued—"something doesn't seem quite right. I just can't put my finger on it."

By this time, Birch had warmed up to Martin enough to

share his thoughts. "The Shirleys have never killed anyone in a bank robbery before. I suppose whenever a bandit waves a gun, there's a good chance someone's going to get hurt eventually."

"That's why Valentine and Rhodes hired you, I guess. They don't want any more killings. They both own a couple of smaller banks in the mining towns along the American River. I think they're afraid that one of their other banks will be held up next."

Platters of food arrived and were plunked unceremoniously down in front of them. The plates contained plenty of beans, boiled beef, and bacon. A basket stuffed with steaming hot sourdough biscuits was set down between the two men, plus a small plate of something that was fried. It took a moment, but Birch finally figured out what it was.

"Hope you like Rocky Mountain 'oysters,' " Molly said, confirming his suspicions.

"Great, Molly," Sheriff Martin said, enthusiastically spearing a couple of them. Rocky Mountain "oysters" were considered a delicacy among many folks out west, but Birch had never acquired a taste for them. He grabbed a hot biscuit instead, then dug into his plate.

Two cups filled with hot black coffee were placed on the table beside them as well. Molly stepped back and, for a moment, watched her customers plow into the food. "I'll be back with more coffee and pie later," she said before she left the dining room.

Both men ate in silence. Birch hadn't realized just how hungry he'd been until the food arrived. The whiskey Molly had served them before the meal had just whetted his appetite. When Birch was finished, he sat back and drank the last of his coffee. The sheriff was still wiping up the gravy on the oyster plate with his last biscuit.

Molly came in carrying a tray. Two slabs of custard pie rested on it next to a coffee pot.

"Those are the finest 'oysters' I've ever eaten," the lawman told her. Birch was amused that Martin hadn't noticed that he'd polished off the plate of delicacies all by himself.

"That's 'cause I always stir a little whiskey in the pan while the fritters is popping," she explained as she set down the huge slabs of custard pie and poured more coffee.

When she left, Martin sat back and sighed. "I'd marry that woman in a minute for her cooking but . . ."

Birch waited, then ventured, "But you're married already?"

The sheriff laughed and nodded. "Yeah. Just as well that I am married. If I wasn't, Molly's husband'd come after me with a shotgun."

Birch smiled. He was anxious to get back to business, but the pie was too tempting. When their plates were clean and they were sitting back in their chairs, drinking their coffee, Birch finally brought up the subject of the robberies again.

"How much money was taken in each robbery?"

The sheriff answered promptly. "Two thousand five hundred dollars here. I think it was over one thousand in Nevada City. Ask Marshal McManus there to get an exact amount."

"That's a lot of money," Birch observed.

Sheriff Martin cleared his throat and looked away for a moment, then said, "Well, you see, Grass Valley is one of the stops along the way."

"Along the way to where?"

The sheriff looked straight at Birch and replied, "The stagecoach with the railroad payroll stops here and at Nevada City. The money is kept overnight, then picked up the next day by a railroad employee."

"Why does the railroad send their money by stagecoach?" Birch asked.

"They're still laying track from Sacramento through some of the bigger mining towns around here, and they'll eventually lay track into Nevada," the sheriff explained. "So they need to give the workers their wages, and the only way to do it is by stagecoach right now."

"If Grass Valley and Nevada City are only ten miles apart, why do some payrolls get dropped here and some in Nevada City?"

"Central Pacific splits just south of us. It's easier for the Dutch Flat workers to pick up their payroll in Nevada City. The workers to the south pick up their payroll here in Grass Valley."

"Was the Nevada City Bank robbed while a payroll was waiting there?"

The sheriff nodded.

Birch continued, "Where else have the Shirleys been spotted?"

"Up and down the American River in some of the mining towns that have sprung up in the last few years. There was also a report that they'd been in a saloon fight in Sierra City, but by the time the law got there, the Shirleys were gone."

"No one has any idea of where the gang might hide out after a robbery?" Birch asked.

"Somewhere in the hills. I don't think it's any one place. I think they know those hills like the back of their hand, sort of like the hills of Kentucky."

Birch finished his coffee and stood up, reaching into his pocket to pay for his meal.

Sheriff Martin followed suit, but stopped Birch paying for his own dinner. "This one's on me. I hope you catch those bastards before they kill someone else."

Birch reached for his hat and said, "I don't know as much about the hills as the Shirleys, but I know something about outlaws. I may need some help with the tracking. Do you know anyone around here who's worth a damn?"

Sheriff Martin plunked his hat on his big head. "I can't think of someone right off. Maybe you'd better talk to Mr. Valentine. He might have some ideas."

CHAPTER 4

BACK at the sheriff's office, Sheriff Martin handed Birch a wanted poster with a description of the Shirley gang. The information was sketchy at best, but he learned some useful facts about the Shirleys. There were four of them: Vardis, Fergis, Homer, and Clyde. Vardis was considered the leader. He was described as having a dark beard and sometimes wore a fringed buckskin jacket. Names were not attached to individual descriptions, other than Vardis. One brother had a large shapeless hat with strips of leather wound around it with feathers and beads. Another brother walked with a marked limp. The fourth was described as portly. No one seemed to know which description fit which brother; still, this was a good beginning for Birch.

Sheriff Martin interrupted. "Anything there that might be useful to you?"

Birch shrugged and handed the poster back. "Maybe. The outlaws could discard the buckskin jacket and the unusual hat at a moment's notice, and the fat brother can lose some weight, but the brother with the limp can't change that." Birch glanced at the handbill and grimaced. "But it's still not much to go on. I don't suppose there's any place or any town that the Shirleys might visit more frequently than most towns."

The big lawman shook his head. "None that I know of. But there has to be someone out there who knows something about the Shirleys. Until you suggested it by asking me all those questions over at Molly's, I hadn't thought of it before."

"What do you mean?" Birch asked.

"Someone had to tell them about those payrolls. They struck twice before, and if I check some of the other banks that have been held up by the Shirleys, I bet I'll find that those banks had some kind of special payroll coming in, too."

Birch felt a mixture of hope and relief. Finally, a real clue. He'd been having visions of spending his days and nights wandering aimlessly through the hills, trying to pick up a trail on these mountain folk.

"So you're planning to contact some of the other banks then?" Birch asked.

Sheriff Martin nodded shortly. "Seems like a good idea. At least I'll feel like I'm doing something. When I get the results, I'll let you know."

"Thanks. I appreciate that." Birch adjusted the brim of his hat and headed for the door.

"Where you going now?" the lawman called after him.

"Going to see my client," was Birch's reply before leaving.

Finding the Grass Valley Bank was easy. It was a large building that stood separately from the buildings on both sides. Most of the structures were built to stand so close together that a mosquito couldn't fly between them. But the bank, painted white with a molded piece at the top of the front of the building, had been built to stand proudly apart. The doors were a bright red, and the lettering above the door that announced to the patron that he was now entering the Grass Valley Bank was also painted in red.

The noise from the street melted away when Birch stepped inside. As he looked around at the hushed mahogany and brass interior, Birch got the idea that everything was conducted in hushed tones to match the decor. He was approached by a timid bank clerk who, in a hushed tone, asked, "May I be of service to you, sir?"

He was a rabbity little man, standing a shade over five feet tall, with hair neatly parted in the middle. The only thing that stood out about him was his hair; it was red, as bright as the Grass Valley Bank doors.

Few people would think to call Birch "sir." He was uncomfortable with that status, but most likely it would just make the nervous clerk more upset if Birch told him that he hated being called sir. So he explained, "I'm here to see Mr. Valentine. Tell him Jefferson Birch has come to ask him a few questions."

The clerk's eyes widened and he rushed on, "Oh, no one sees Mr. Valentine, sir. Not without an appointment. Do you have an appointment?" He appeared to be out of breath by the time he had finished.

"No. No appointment. But I think Mr. Valentine would want to see me," Birch said easily.

The clerk drew himself up to his full height and said in a cold tone, "I really am sorry, sir, but—" He was unable to finish his sentence.

Birch came up close to him and said evenly, "Tell Mr. Valentine that Jefferson Birch from Tisdale Investigations is here regarding the bank robbery."

The clerk stood there for a minute, his mouth gaping open, then he spun on his heel and walked away. A few minutes later, he came back and ushered Birch into Mr. Valentine's office. A large oak desk, three chairs, and an oak file cabinet were the only pieces of furniture in the stark room. A Rochester brass bowl lamp sat on the desk next to the green blotter. It was much more modest an office than what Birch had expected from a bank owner.

Harold Valentine stood up and extended his hand as Birch entered the office. "Mr. Birch. I understand that you're Arthur Tisdale's agent. I trust you had a pleasant journey."

Birch was sure that Valentine wasn't at all interested in his journey north. He took his hat off, shook the bank owner's hand, and sat in a chair facing his client across the desk. Birch studied Harold Valentine. He was a man of medium height with slicked-down brown hair, a cleft chin, and wire-rim glasses perched on a sharp nose. He wore a well-starched white linen shirt and a black broadcloth suit. A large gold railroad watch was draped across his black vest, and gold cuff links were in his paper cuffs.

"I suppose you'd like to know why you've been brought down here. From what Mr. Tisdale relayed to me, I understand that you were summoned rather suddenly from Modesto."

Birch inclined his head and said, "I have learned a few things about the case. I just came from the sheriff's office."

"I see," Valentine replied, raising his eyebrows. "You don't waste time, do you?"

"I needed to find out about the gang that has been accused of robbing the banks around here," Birch said, adding, "I was also deputized, which makes my work easier." He displayed his deputy badge. The bank owner smiled wryly.

"And what conclusion have you drawn?" Valentine asked. Birch noticed that he talked in a formal manner.

"I think the Shirleys are a good bet. Sheriff Martin has offered to find out what other banks have been hit in the area."

Valentine leaned forward in his chair, his interest sparked. "Why?"

Birch hesitated for a moment, then said, "There may be someone outside of the Shirleys who is giving them information. Both your bank and the one in Nevada City were robbed at a time when you had a railroad payroll in the safe. It may be a coincidence, but I don't think so."

Valentine nodded. "I see. And you're certain that the Shirley gang was involved?"

"I didn't say that," Birch replied shortly. "I said that the

Shirleys were a good bet. There is one thing that bothers me."

Valentine sat back slightly and rested the tips of his fingers, tentlike, on his chin. "And what is it that bothers you?"

Birch replied, "There was a murder at the Nevada City Bank. The Shirleys have never killed anyone before."

"Is that significant?" Valentine asked.

"I don't know yet. But I'd like to investigate some other possibilities if I think it's necessary."

Valentine suddenly stood up and leaned over his desk, possibly in an effort to intimidate Birch, and said in a low, fierce voice, "Just find them and bring them in, Birch."

This was the first time he had displayed any emotion about the robberies since Birch had been ushered into the office.

"If you want the bank robbers, you have to let me lead my own investigation," Birch replied. "If you just want someone arrested to hang the blame on, get another man." He started to get up from his chair. Valentine gestured to him to stay. Birch sat back down.

Sighing wearily, the bank owner said, "You're right. I'm jumping to conclusions. What do you need?"

"Information."

Valentine nodded. "Go ahead."

"I want a list of everyone who knows about the payroll schedule here in Grass Valley."

The bank owner furrowed his brow in thought. "That's not many people. Not even my clerk or tellers know when it'll come in until the afternoon before, but that doesn't mean someone couldn't figure it out."

"So you're the only one who would know?"

"Me, Sheriff Martin, the stagecoach driver, the railroad employee who sends the money to us . . ." Valentine's voice trailed off for a moment, then replied, "That's it. I can vouch for Sheriff Martin. The man is above reproach. Is there anything else you need to know?"

"Not at the moment," Birch said. He started to stand. "Oh, there is one more thing. I may need to bring another man into this case."

"Someone else?" Valentine repeated in a scandalized tone. "Surely you can handle this investigation by yourself, Mr. Birch."

Birch sighed and replied, "I can handle the investigation fine. When it comes to tracking the Shirleys, I'll need some help."

"There are plenty of people to choose from in Grass Valley," the bank owner assured Birch. "I'm sure that Sheriff Martin will be more than happy to recommend someone."

Birch shook his head. "I've been thinking about it, Mr. Valentine. We need someone from outside this area. Someone above reproach." He imitated the phrase he'd heard Valentine use earlier.

Valentine slowly nodded his head as he thought about what Birch had said. "Yes, that might be better. All right. I hereby authorize you to bring another agent into this investigation. I trust that this man is someone you know very well."

Birch nodded, not wanting to admit that he had no idea who he had in mind. He grabbed his hat, shook hands with his client one more time, and left the bank.

Walking down Grass Valley's main street, Birch turned the matter over in his head. When no name came to mind, he turned into the first saloon he came across. It was called Duffy's and was better than what he was used to.

Feeling a bit out of place, Birch ordered a double whiskey. A sign on the mirror above the backbar caught his eye: MISS LULU MONTANA WILL PERFORM A REPERTOIRE OF SONGS THIS SATURDAY NIGHT. He sipped the whiskey that had been placed in front of him only a moment ago and looked around, wondering who he could call on. Birch dismissed Arthur Tisdale as a possibility. His boss might have been an old cavalry man, but Birch didn't think Tisdale could find a herd of cows in a pasture without a map.

There was the young ranch hand in Carson City, Clem Johnston, who had been accused of killing his boss. Birch had proven his innocence and found the real killer. He discarded that notion, telling himself that Johnston was too young and probably didn't have the experience needed.

Besides, Birch had courted Johnston's sister, Emma, for a few months before she met and married a small rancher in the area. During their courtship, Emma had made it clear that she wanted to stay in and around Carson City. Birch wasn't sure that was where he wanted to settle down. Although their parting had been mutual and friendly, Birch still felt a little uncomfortable with the idea of working with Emma's brother so soon afterward.

Birch signaled for another whiskey. While he was waiting for it, a large man burst through the saloon doors, walked up to the bar, and pounded on the surface for service.

"Bartender!" he bellowed. "A drink."

Birch's whiskey was placed in front of him so quickly that the bartender didn't even stay to make sure he was paid. Instead, the saloon keeper grabbed a bottle of red-eye and a glass and went over to the new customer, a tough-looking man with rolled-up sleeves. As the bartender poured, he said, "You ain't gonna bust up my place like you did last week, are you, Walt?"

Walt laughed. "You know I don't start fights, Frank. It's those young ones who get a few drinks in 'em, then think they can take me on."

Birch eavesdropped with amusement. The big man,

Walt, reminded him of a logger he once knew, someone who was now marshal of a small boomtown in Oregon. Swede.

He tossed the rest of his whiskey down, laid a coin on the bar, and headed for the telegraph office. He needed to send a wire to Grant's Pass, Oregon.

CHAPTER 5

THE next day, Birch received a wire confirming that Swede would be arriving in Grass Valley in a few days. Birch estimated that it would take Swede at least two days by train to get to Sacramento, then another day by stagecoach to get to Grass Valley. Meanwhile, Birch would continue to ask questions and poke around until he found a few leads.

It seemed only logical for Birch to ride into Nevada City the next morning to talk to the other bank owner, Vernon Rhodes, and the eyewitness. As Birch approached the town, he paused at the crest of a hill and stared beyond the cluster of buildings below that made up Nevada City. Shrouded in purple mist, the Sierras rose up like an impenetrable wall beyond the boomtown. To the north and south of Nevada City, great waves of lush green hills undulated as far as the eye could see.

With a population of several thousand, Nevada City was only slightly smaller than Grass Valley. As Birch rode slowly down the main street to give Cactus a rest, he noted that there were five saloons for every church; houses small and plain, others large and grandiose, dotted the low hilly areas behind the saloons, general stores, and hotels that lined both sides of the main street. The foothills of the distant mountains looked like giants' feet to Birch.

Although he was hungry, thirsty, tired, and felt grimy, duty came before pleasure and comfort. So he opted to look for the local lawman. Birch's past experience spurred him to find the marshal as soon as he got into town, if he was there on business. Amid the clattering hooves and squeaking buggy wheels, Birch spotted the marshal's office, reined in Cactus, and dismounted. As he stepped up on the boardwalk and got closer, he spied a hastily scrawled note, pinned to the door. "Be back soon," it read. Probably written on the back of a wanted poster, Birch mused.

He stepped back from the door and looked around, wondering whether to wait or find a room. People walked by hastily without paying him any attention. Birch noticed a drinking trough across the street, so he led Cactus to it. As the horse noisily lapped up his fill, Birch kept watch on the marshal's office.

"He might not be back till later this afternoon," a voice spoke behind him. Birch turned to face a mild-looking man with muttonchops and a severe part down the middle of his greased hair. A dark blue vest covered most of the well-starched white cotton shirt. Black garters fastened and held his sleeves in place. He nervously tapped a pencil against his clean-shaven chin, shifted from one foot to the other, and explained, "I saw you go up to his office a few minutes ago. I work in the assay office. The name's Earl Dunlap." He gestured to the assay sign behind him. "You were looking for the marshal, weren't you?"

Birch nodded. "Maybe you could direct me to a place where I could get a room and a bath. Seems the most sensible thing for me to do while waiting for the marshal to get back."

Dunlap replied hastily, "Oh, very sensible. You look like you've been traveling a great distance, stranger. If you keep going down the street, there's a couple of hotels to choose from. And there are a few boarding houses off in that direction," he said, waving vaguely to the south and added, "if you'd prefer."

Birch touched his hat. "Thanks. Much obliged."

"If I see Marshal McManus before you get back here," Dunlap replied, "should I tell him anything special?"

"Tell him Jefferson Birch is looking for him."

"Birch?" Dunlap squinted at him. "Say, are you the fella who was hired by Vernon Rhodes? You're looking into the bank robbery."

Birch nodded and looked uncomfortable. "That's right." He didn't like the notion that everyone in a town knew who he was and why he was there. His job was easier if he could catch people off guard so that they would tell him things that they might not normally confide.

"Say, I was here when the robbery happened." Dunlap puffed out his chest and continued, "I was one of the first people out the door when we heard that shot."

"Would you tell me how it happened?" Birch asked.

"Well, it was just a normal summer day a few weeks ago. A customer had just come in to get my report on some nuggets he found on his claim and—"

"You came out of your office when you heard the shots," Birch prompted.

"Yes. Marshal McManus was already outside and facing in the direction of the bank. Well, naturally I turned that way, too, and was able to make out a figure running toward us, arms flailing, yelling something. But we couldn't hear what he was saying, or see who he was, until he got closer. I was the first one to recognize Cyrus Dundee, the bank clerk. And then we heard him yelling that the bank had been robbed and Joe Child had been shot. That's when the deputy came out to see what was going on and the marshal started shouting orders. Then the deputy got a posse together. I was one of the volunteers."

"Did you pick up the trail of the robbers?" Birch asked.

Earl Dunlap shook his head sadly. "No, we tried, but by the time the posse was together and heading out of town, we must have been too late. There's a lot of travelers on the road out of town just beyond the bank. We kept looking for some sign. The trail was so dry and dusty that day that a wagon train could have passed by and we wouldn't have been able to tell."

"Is there anything else you can tell me?"

Dunlap shook his head. "I guess that wasn't very much, was it?" he said. "You know, I had some savings in the bank. Vernon Rhodes has said he would try to make up for the stolen money, but if it's gone, it's gone." He shrugged.

"I appreciate your version of the robbery, Mr. Dunlap," Birch replied. "Whether you know it or not, you've been a help." He got on his horse and tipped his hat to the assay clerk. "Thanks again."

With that, Birch wheeled Cactus around and headed in the direction Dunlap had pointed a moment ago.

Two hours later in his room, a well-scrubbed Birch donned his clean black cotton shirt, black broadcloth trousers and coat. He had chosen a hotel because he wanted a bath as soon as possible and if he'd stayed at a boarding house, he would probably have had to wait until after supper, then he couldn't be certain that he'd get clean water. Sometimes a boarder could be the third or fourth to use the bathwater, and by then, it wouldn't be hot anymore. From his past experience, Birch found that hotels were much more accommodating.

Peering into the blotchy silvered mirror, he ran a comb through his wet, slicked-back hair. Then he ran a hand over his two-day stubble. He wouldn't mind visiting a barber and getting a meal—not necessarily in that order— but it would have to wait until Birch had talked to the marshal. Birch strapped on his gun belt and left the hotel.

This time he walked to the marshal's office, taking in the sights, sounds, and smells of Nevada City. A black man wearing a grubby pair of overalls swept the sidewalk outside of a supply store.

Two little urchins, probably a brother and sister, stood in front of a general store with their faces pressed against the glass. Rows of glass candy jars lined the back shelves, and the boy and girl were staring intently at the licorice whips and peppermints. Birch paused, dug out a penny, and handed it to the girl, who appeared to be the older of the two.

"Thanks, mister!" she smiled, turning and punching her brother on the shoulder. He looked over, his eyes widening when he saw the penny. With big grins on their faces, they ran into the store to satisfy their sweet tooth. Birch smiled after them. The boy could be no more than four years old, just about the age that his infant son would have been, had he lived. He tore himself away from the sight, turning his mind to the task at hand.

He passed a barber shop, then a small restaurant called Alma's Place. His stomach growled, reminding Birch that he hadn't eaten since early morning. That was getting to be a bad habit. He quickened his pace, intent on handing over his letter of introduction to the marshal and discussing the case.

The note had been taken down and Birch entered the office. At one end of the room, a chubby, baby-faced deputy was paring his nails with a penknife, his hat jammed crookedly on his head. He sat behind a desk, his wooden chair groaning with the weight and instability of being tipped back on two legs. The deputy's boots rested comfortably on the scarred desk surface. When he noticed Birch, a startled look crossed his face, and he sat up much too quickly, stabbing one of his fingers with the knife in the process.

He cursed and shook his hand, finally settling on sucking his wounded finger, then wrapping it up in his bandanna. "Can I help you?" he asked Birch.

"When will the marshal be back?" Birch asked.

The deputy looked at Birch with open curiosity and replied, "Guess he won't be back till later tonight. Might not be back till tomorrow. What can I do for you?"

Birch hesitated. He didn't like to bring up official business to a deputy before he'd had a chance to talk to the marshal. Although many lawmen didn't mind if their deputies were given information before they were, there were plenty who would take it as a personal insult.

The deputy seemed to sense Birch's uneasiness. "Look, the marshal had to settle a dispute east of here. That's several hours' ride for him. If he gets back tonight, he probably won't be in any mood for whatever you're here to talk to him about. Why don't you tell me about it."

That decided Birch. There was no use putting off what needed to be started today. Birch wanted to make sure he was back in Grass Valley by Saturday to meet Swede's stagecoach. It was a good thing that the railroad had built tracks up north through Grant's Pass about a year ago. It made Swede's trip down to Grass Valley much faster than it might have been by horse.

Birch pulled out the letter of introduction that Tisdale had sent him and handed it to the deputy. "My name is Jefferson Birch and your marshal should be expecting me. I'm here to investigate the bank robberies."

The deputy glanced at the letter, put it on his desk, and stood up. "Yeah, I heard you was comin' here. The marshal told me." A cloud passed over his face at the mention of his boss, then quickly was replaced by a smile. "Sure am glad you're here, Mr. Birch. My name's Jim Wells."

Birch shook Wells's hand. "Then you won't mind my poking around, asking questions? I was deputized by Sheriff Martin, if that makes a difference." He flashed the star, which he wore pinned to his shirt under his coat.

Wells shrugged. "Heck, I'm just glad someone's here to help. The marshal's been kind of hard to live with ever since the robbery. Seems to blame himself for Joe Child's death." Wells took his hat off and scratched his forehead. "So I suppose you need to talk to the eyewitness."

Birch nodded. "Can you tell me his name?"

"Cyrus Dundee. One of the bank tellers. Actually, now he's the only one there. Mr. Rhodes hasn't taken on anyone else yet. He's been working at the teller window himself lately."

"Mr. Rhodes is the other bank owner who hired me," Birch said.

"That's what I heard from Ty," Wells replied, quickly adding, "Tyrell McManus is the name of the marshal here."

"I'll need to get started while I'm down here. I have to be back in Grass Valley the day after tomorrow, so since Marshal McManus isn't here, would it be all right if I ask around?"

"Long as you don't go getting yourself in any fights." The deputy picked up the letter again and studied it for a moment. "Says here you used to ride with the Rangers in Texas." He looked up, his eyes burning with interest.

Birch inclined his head. "Five years with them." He didn't like to talk much about it. Memories of his dead wife, Audrey, and baby son invariably haunted him when Birch's past was dredged up.

Wells shook his head slightly and commented, "That must have really been something. That's what I want to do. What was it like? Did you fight a lot of Mexicans and Indians?"

Birch tried to focus on the deputy's questions instead of on his own memory of the last mission he'd been sent on. "It'll take you a day at most," his captain had assured him. "You should be back in plenty of time to be with your wife and baby."

It had taken much longer to negotiate with the officials to get back the horse thieves who had crossed the Rio Grande into Mexico. Birch returned to his ranch the day after the funeral, and all he could do was stand beside the freshly filled-in graves, his hat in his hand, his heart buried six feet deep with Audrey and the son who had lived only a few hours.

"There was some of that," he replied to the deputy. "But mostly we rounded up rustlers. Sometimes there were murderers to go after. We captured a couple of gangs down there, too, but it wasn't always fighting."

Wells nodded slowly. Birch thought he saw disappointment in the deputy's eyes.

"Well, you go ahead and do what you gotta do," the deputy said, adjusting his hat on his head. "I'll let McManus know that you're here, and if you need anything from us, just let me know."

"You were here when the bank was robbed?"

"Yeah, I was here in the office. We heard the gunshot, then Cyrus Dundee came running toward us like hell was on his heels. He was flailing his arms at us and yelling."

"What was he yelling?"

"Oh, what anyone would say. 'The bank's been robbed, Joe Child is shot,' he kept saying over and over."

"Did you say you only heard one gunshot?"

"That's right."

"And did you go to the bank?"

Wells shook his head. "Naw. The marshal went. He ordered me to go find the doctor and organize a posse. It took a while because a couple of volunteers had to saddle their horses."

"How long?"

"About fifteen or twenty minutes."

Birch rubbed his whiskered jaw and thought about it. "Did you pick up their tracks?"

Wells looked downcast for a moment. "Naw. We lost them in the hills."

"So Cyrus was the only one who saw them, and he's sure it's the Shirley gang," Birch said.

"Yeah, he's sure. He picked out their wanted poster and described them almost exactly like what was written down there." The deputy moved to the other desk and said, "Here. I'll show you the poster." He pulled a crumpled piece of paper out of the top drawer and handed it to Birch.

"Sheriff Martin already showed me one of these. But thanks," he replied, handing it back to Wells.

The deputy looked slightly disappointed as he returned the poster to the marshal's desk drawer. Birch's stomach rumbled, an impatient reminder that he hadn't yet eaten.

He headed for the door. "Thanks for your help, Deputy."

"Come by any time," the deputy said in an eager voice. "If you need anything or have any more questions, I'll do my best."

Birch had his hand on the knob, anxious to leave. He wanted to ask the deputy how the food at Alma's Place was, but he was afraid Wells would want to join him so he could hear more about the Rangers.

Out on the street again, he headed for the sign that promised him a meal. Once inside, a thin humorless woman waited on him.

"What do you want?" she asked flatly.

If Birch hadn't already sat down, he'd have left and found another place. As he ordered, he thought about Molly's little dining room off her saloon back in Grass Valley and wished he were there right now. As he waited for his steak and potatoes, he looked around. There were a couple of plain wooden tables with plain wooden chairs for the customers to sit at while they enjoyed their meal. There were no decorations, no paint on the walls, not even a reproduction of a picture torn from a magazine or newspaper. The place was as sterile as a hospital, but without the charity.

All he wanted was good plain food, but when his meal arrived, the steak was tough and the biscuits tougher. The mashed potatoes were lumpy and the gravy was watery.

Still, Birch tucked into his meal to satisfy his hunger, and it was only when he looked up that he realized he was the only customer in the place. After refusing a second cup of Alma's weak coffee, Birch paid for his meal. By his way of thinking, he'd already paid by eating it. But he grudgingly compensated the lady for taking the trouble to ruin good food. Then he left the restaurant, never to darken its doors again—as he was certain happened to most of the customers who came here once.

Out on the street again, Birch wasn't sure in which direction the Nevada City Bank was located. He stopped a black cowboy dressed in dusty ranch clothes and was pointed in the opposite direction.

When he arrived outside the bank, he took a little time to notice that the building sat on the edge of town. He remembered that Earl Dunlap had told him that the bank was convenient to travelers coming into or going out of Nevada City. Once inside, he noticed how quiet it was. The temperature was cooler as well.

A portly, red-faced man approached him. "Can I help you, sir?" he puffed. The effort of talking and walking was apparently too much of a strain on his soft body. "Perhaps you'd care to open an account with us?"

"No, actually, I'd like to talk to the bank owner, Vernon Rhodes."

"That's me," the man replied warily.

Birch introduced himself, handing over his letter of introduction for the third time. Vernon Rhodes read it slowly, occasionally muttering something to himself. Finally, he looked up, perspiration beading his upper lip. "This is very impressive, Mr. Birch." He glanced down at the letter again to reassure himself and repeated, "Very impressive." After handing back the letter to Birch, Rhodes held out a plump, moist hand. Birch shook it, then wiped his hand on the side of his broadcloth coat while Rhodes led him back to his office.

"We can talk better in here, I think," Rhodes explained as he closed the door.

Birch hadn't gotten more than a glimpse of the eyewitness, Cyrus Dundee. His impression was of a slight, timid man with bifocals. Birch began to have doubts that anyone with glasses that thick could have seen anything, let alone be able to identify a whole gang. However, Dundee was the only witness to the robbery and killing, so he would have to do.

Rhodes sat behind a large, imposing desk. "Now then, let's get down to business, shall we?"

CHAPTER 6

VERNON Rhodes had very little to add regarding the robbery, as Birch soon found out. The bank owner had been at home with his wife, taking a noon meal, while his bank was being robbed.

"Can you tell me what happened after you were told about the robbery?" Birch asked.

Rhodes frowned and puffed out his cheeks in thought. "I ran over here as fast as I could."

Considering how stout the bank owner was, Birch didn't think that would have been very fast.

"When I got here," Rhodes continued, "the marshal and Cyrus Dundee were here. The doctor had already come and gone, since Joe Child was dead." He paused and grunted, then leaned forward, his pudgy hands clasped together, and said, "Tell me what you've come up with so far, Mr. Birch."

Birch had taken off his black hat upon entering the mahogany and leather room. He ran a hand through his light brown hair, a twisted smile on his face as he replied, "I don't have much at this point," adding, in a sardonic tone, "I haven't caught the outlaws, if that's what you mean."

Rhodes frowned impatiently. "Why did you want to see me then?"

"I came here to introduce myself to you and to find out if there's anything you think I should know before I proceed. I also want to talk to your eyewitness."

"He's at your disposal," Rhodes said, waving a hand in a gesture of dismissal. "Of course, the marshal has already talked to Cyrus, who identified the gang who robbed my bank." Rhodes added, "That's why I'm cooperating with Harold Valentine. Our banks were robbed by the same men."

"Weren't there some other banks in the area that were robbed by the Shirley gang as well?" Birch asked.

Rhodes concurred by bobbing his head up and down like a large red apple in a pail of water. "Yes, a number of banks were robbed by the Shirleys over the last three years. Harold and I contacted a few of them with the idea of hiring you, but they all declined. I guess they figured what was done was done." He opened a wooden cigar box and took out a cigar. Hesitating just a bit, he shoved the box toward Birch and asked, "You want one? They're from Cuba." He cut one end off and stuck it in his mouth. Birch declined politely. He'd never cared much for the taste of tobacco.

Rhodes picked up a small statue of a soldier smoking a cigar and flicked the switch on its back. A flame burst out of the end of the small cigar replica and Rhodes lit up his larger version. After a few puffs to get it going, during which he studied Birch in silence, Rhodes asked, "After talking to my clerk, how do you intend to proceed with the investigation?" He pointed his cigar at Birch and added, "I want these sons-of-bitches caught for robbing my bank, but I don't want you drawing out the investigation so you can make more money."

Birch hadn't been sure what to think of Rhodes, but he now concluded that he was contemptible. There had been no mention of the death of his former employee, Joe Child, except in passing. He was more concerned with his business and with capturing the bank robbers.

Birch made a conscious decision to have as little contact with Rhodes as possible. He was thankful that he was stationed in Grass Valley. At least Harold Valentine was a more reasonable man.

"I'm glad you feel that way, Mr. Rhodes, because I've taken steps to get this investigation under way. I've hired another man to work with me and he should be arriving in Grass Valley on Saturday."

The bank owner's face turned purple, and he started choking. "Wha—?" Rhodes's question was interrupted as he began hacking. Birch watched with malicious pleasure. Finally, the bank owner stopped coughing and said, "What do you mean, you've hired someone else? You need permission to do that and I haven't given it."

"No," Birch replied calmly, "but Mr. Valentine has. I explained to him that when the time came to track down the outlaws, a second man would be a good idea."

"But—but," Rhodes sputtered, "we'd have to pay him. And what is this about the second man arriving in Grass Valley? Where is he coming from?"

"Oregon."

"Oregon?" Rhodes repeated in disbelief. "Why not hire someone from around here?"

Birch explained to his client the need to hire someone who was beyond suspicion. As he launched into an account of his meeting with Valentine the other day, Rhodes's expression relaxed. Toward the end, he was beaming and nodding in agreement. "You're quite right, Birch. I didn't think of it that way. Someone must be supplying information to these outlaws." He frowned again, this time in thought. "But it can't be the law. Both McManus here in Nevada City and Martin in Grass Valley are above reproach, men like yourself." Rhodes had risen from his chair by now and walked around his desk to stand near Birch. He took the opportunity to clap Birch on the back to emphasize his point.

Birch remained silent as Rhodes continued. "And I know it wasn't Valentine or myself. Why would either of us hire you if that were the case. No, it has to be someone else. We can't be the only ones to know about the payroll."

"There are the stagecoach drivers," Birch offered.

The bank owner seized on this suggestion with enthusiasm. "Yes, it could be! What about the railroad employees who send it out? And the ones who receive it? You've got a lot of possibilities to work with."

Too many, Birch thought grimly. He had to narrow down the choices when he got a chance. The first thing he'd do when he got back to Grass Valley would be to find out from the sheriff if the other banks had been robbed during a large payroll. Then he'd look for the connection. But for now, he didn't want to discuss all of the possibilities with Rhodes. He wanted to talk to Cyrus Dundee.

Their talk concluded, Rhodes agreed to send Cyrus Dundee in while he watched the bank. A few minutes after the bank owner left, a meek-looking man crept into the office, closing the door quietly. Cyrus Dundee wore thick bifocals, and what was left of his wispy light hair clung precariously to his egg-shaped head. With a linen handkerchief, he patted at the beads of perspiration on his forehead. Birch had to get closer to see that Dundee was trying to grow a mustache, but his efforts had paid off in a few straggly blond hairs that looked as if he'd forgotten to shave.

Dundee cleared his throat. "You must be Mr. Birch," he said, holding out a hand, a tentative look on his face. "I'm afraid that I've gone through this over and over again with the marshal, and every night when I try to get to sleep. But I can't think of anything new I could add to what I saw. I guess I'm just not very observant." His thin shoulders slumped as if in defeat.

"I'd like to hear your story from the beginning. I haven't talked to Marshal McManus yet, but I'll get information from him soon enough."

When Dundee was finished telling his account, Birch felt let down. There wasn't anything new in his description of what happened that Birch couldn't have figured out for

himself. Birch asked a few questions, trying to prompt the
bank clerk's memory, but it was a half-hearted attempt at
best. He kept going back to the description of the bank
robbers, asking Dundee if he was sure it was the Shirleys
who robbed the bank. But Dundee held fast.

The bank clerk was trembling by the time Birch ran out
of questions. Dundee was fiddling with a pencil that he'd
taken from Rhodes's desk. "Is that all, Mr. Birch?" Dundee
asked meekly. "I mean, can I go now? I hate to leave Mr.
Rhodes out there for very long. For a bank owner, he can't
balance figures very well."

Birch sighed, feeling defeated. He rubbed the back of
his neck and replied, "For now. But I may have a few more
questions to ask before I leave."

Cyrus Dundee nodded, put the pencil carefully back on
the desk, and got up, obviously anxious to go. He paused
at the open door and said, "I wish I had more to tell you,
Mr. Birch. Sometimes I wish I'd been here during the
robbery. Maybe I could have done something."

Birch looked at the timid man and smiled wearily. "If
you had been there, you might have been shot along with
Joe Child."

"I guess you're right, Mr. Birch," Dundee replied
thoughtfully, then shook his head sadly. "Poor Kathleen.
She's taken Joe's death so hard."

"Joe Child's wife?" Birch asked.

Cyrus Dundee nodded sadly. "Is there anything else,
Mr. Birch? I'd like to get back in there."

Birch stood up and walked toward Dundee. "Maybe you
can help more. Show me where Joe was and how the
outlaws got out."

He followed Dundee to the back of the bank. "This is
where I found Joe, after I heard the shot." Dundee indicated an area near the safe. Out of the corner of his eye,
Birch could see Rhodes watching them with interest.

"All right. Now where were you?" Birch asked.

"I was just outside that door," Dundee said, pointing to the side door on the other side of the back room. He walked over to it and opened it up. Birch could see the side of the next building through the open door. "This is the way bank employees enter in the morning and at noon. And we leave this way at night," Cyrus Dundee explained as he shut the door. "As I said, I heard the shot from outside and then I came in. Joe was lying there and I heard the sound of horses out front. I ran to the door and opened it in time to see four riders leaving. Then I ran toward the marshal's office."

Rhodes could no longer keep quiet. He added, "The safe was open when I arrived. I thought only Cyrus and myself had the combination, but from what Cyrus told us on the day of the robbery, I guess Joe knew where I kept the slip of paper with the numbers," Rhodes explained, looking sheepish as he related this to Birch. He continued, "All the money drawers were open, and Joe was lying facedown on the floor over here." He walked over to the side door.

Birch frowned and walked over to the door, then turned and looked at the rest of the room. Something about the robbery was bothering him, but he couldn't quite put his finger on it.

Cyrus Dundee scurried up to Rhodes to consult with him about some figures. Birch strode over to the safe and studied it. He'd seen safes like this one before. There was no doubt that the teller must have been forced to open it. Although there were a few outlaws who no doubt could crack the combination, it would take time and patience. From what Birch had read about the Shirleys, he didn't think any of them had the patience or the intelligence. They were clever enough, but didn't seem very smart. And as for time, he didn't think they would have chanced more than a quick run on the bank in the middle of the afternoon when anyone could have walked in to make a deposit or withdrawal.

Birch opened the door. "You leaving us now?" Rhodes called out.

"I think I've done all I can here for the moment."

"If you think of any other questions, I'm available day or night," Rhodes said eagerly. "When are you going back to Grass Valley?"

Birch thought about it. He'd done just about everything he had to do. "I might leave tomorrow. It depends."

When the formalities were over, Birch left. The sun was hanging low in the sky and the temperature had fallen. Birch looked up and spotted thunderclouds in the sky, off to the west. He put his hat back on and adjusted it so the brim was straight. Then he walked over to the stables to check on Cactus. His horse was doing just fine. He was, at the moment, munching on a bag of oats, looking very content.

As Birch was leaving the stable, a man was walking toward him. Everything about him was average, except for the sun glinting off of the tin badge he wore on his blue cotton shirt. Birch came to the conclusion that this was Marshal McManus. From the look on his face, the meeting wasn't going to be a pleasure.

"Are you Jefferson Birch?" the man snapped, his face flushed with suppressed anger.

Birch kept his face impassive, knowing that a smile at this time could be misinterpreted. "You must be Marshal McManus," he said shortly.

"Enough with the introductions. Back at my office." The lawman turned on his heel and strode back up the street, Birch following at a distance. When they got to the office, the deputy was just coming out the door, a contrite look on his face. As he passed Birch though, he grinned and winked.

"Don't take the marshal's anger too personal," he explained in a low voice. "He's just mad 'cause he didn't get the son-of-a-bitch who killed Joe Child."

Birch nodded his understanding and patted Wells on the shoulder before entering the lion's den. McManus was standing behind his desk, his body leaning over the surface.

"How dare you come into my town and question people without my permission," he began in a low voice. "You could have waited until I got back tonight."

Birch replied in a mild voice, "Can you tell me who I've upset?"

This question took the marshal by surprise. "What do you mean?" he asked bleakly.

"Has anyone come in here to complain about my presence in town?"

"No," came the marshal's weak reply. He tugged at his mustache, seeming to gather momentum again. In a curious tone, he added, "But the letter I received from your employer stated that you would visit my office before launching your investigation."

"And I did," Birch pointed out. "I talked to your deputy. He wasn't sure when you'd be back. I have to be back in Grass Valley by Saturday."

McManus was beginning to slump, his anger spent. He sat heavily in the chair behind him and gestured for Birch to do the same. After they were both seated, the marshal rubbed the bridge of his nose and sighed.

"I apologize for acting like such a fool," he began. "But I guess you'd better know that from the beginning, I've been against the notion of hiring someone from the outside to investigate the robberies."

"Why?" Birch asked.

"I think we can get the Shirleys without your help."

"But how long would it take you to track them down? Remember, you've got a town to look after, too."

McManus took a deep breath and expelled it, puffing up his cheeks as he did so, then reluctantly nodded.

Birch was glad he'd talked to McManus' deputy before meeting the marshal. He had a better understanding of what drove McManus, what made him so angry, and therefore, he didn't take it personally. Birch rested his elbows on the arms of the chair and leaned forward. "Well, I have the time and I have as much experience at this as you do. I'm not trying to take any glory away from you and I don't have a reputation as a gunfighter. I just want to do the job that I was hired for."

There was a pause as Birch waited for the marshal to make the next move. It didn't take long before McManus stuck his hand out. As they shook, Birch felt that there was an unspoken understanding between them.

"Welcome to Nevada City," McManus said, a grin finally spreading across his face. "What can I do to help?"

"You just did it," Birch acknowledged.

CHAPTER 7

BIRCH spent an hour with McManus, asking questions and listening to his description of that day. Although the marshal mentioned Wilmer Colbert and Doc Holder, two men who had come into the bank right after the robbery, Birch didn't think they would be worth the trouble to interview. If he thought it would be necessary later on, he would find them or maybe he would get Swede to talk to them. Birch noticed that whenever the marshal mentioned Joe Child, a troubled frown would cross McManus's face, and he would reach up to absently tug at his mustache.

Birch stood up. "Thank you for your time, Marshal."

Jim Wells came in and raised his eyebrows in amazement. McManus caught the look on the deputy's face and sternly said, "We're both still here, Jim. Birch and I have reached an understanding."

The deputy's face relaxed into a broad grin. "I kind of figured that you'd either have the biggest damn fight this side of the Mississippi or you'd learn to get along. Glad to see you're both in one piece."

Birch put his hat back on and said, "I think that's all I'll need for now. I'll be leaving tomorrow afternoon."

McManus nodded. "You just let me know when you come back and we'll talk again."

Birch took his evening meal at a nearby saloon. He wanted to get an early start back to Grass Valley in the morning. He was eager to meet with Valentine and discuss the bank robberies.

As he was finishing his meal, three miners staggered in and ordered a bottle of whiskey.

"I knew it was a bonanza, Mort," crowed a miner with a blue bandanna.

A second miner, his nose a shapeless mass from losing too many fights, replied, "I always knew you had a nose for gold. Goddamned if you didn't know right where it was."

The third miner, a younger man in his early twenties, looked around cautiously and chided the other two. "Shh. Keep your voices down, you damn fools. You want everyone in this place to know about it?"

Blue Bandanna threw his head back and cackled. Then he picked up his glass in a careless toast, sloshing whiskey all over the table. "Of course we want everyone to know," he boomed at the top of his lungs. The young miner, a pained look on his face, gestured for silence, but Blue Bandanna continued, "We found gold! We're rich! We can afford any damn thing we please. We want a woman. Bartender! Get me a woman. Not just any woman, but a real looker." He tossed his drink down and poured another for himself and his partners.

The bartender looked over at the men, sharply, then turned back to his business behind the bar. He acted as if this sort of customer came in every day. And they probably did.

Blue Bandanna stood up unsteadily and shouted his request again. "Bartend! I said I want a woman. Bring one to me."

This time, the bartender turned and shrugged. "We have only one woman here, sir, and she's my wife."

"What about her?" Blue Bandanna pointed to the back of the room. There was a piano with a man just sitting down. Beside the piano, a woman stood, sheet music in her hand. She was small and delicate like bone china with fine porcelain features, an alabaster complexion, and long, glossy black hair that was pulled up and set in a net with gold tassels and a roll. Brilliant green eyes glittered beneath long, thick lashes. She wore a burgundy satin gown with a wide gold band at her tiny waist. The dress rustled when she bent close to the piano player to consult the sheet music.

The bartender blanched, came out from behind his bar and approached the three miners, stammering, "Th-that's Lulu Montana. She's just the entertainment tonight. I tell you, sir, we have no saloon girls here. Miss Montana is a singer. Please, mister, don't cause any trouble."

Birch remembered that he'd seen her name on a poster in a Grass Valley saloon. She would be playing up there tomorrow night. He looked around and noticed that the place was beginning to fill up. The bartender went back to his station and began filling drink orders.

Birch had intended to leave as soon as he'd finished his meal, but he was intrigued enough to stay and listen to Lulu Montana for a short while. He watched the miners out of the corner of his eye. The other two were trying to console their companion, but Blue Bandanna watched the lithesome singer with a determined look in his eye. Birch overheard snatches of conversation as the young miner tried to convince Blue Bandanna to leave.

"We'll find you a woman, Ernest," the younger miner wheedled. "Why don't we finish this bottle and go over to one of them dance hall saloons and find a hurdy girl for you."

Mort, the miner with the mashed nose, agreed. "Yeah, we could do that. I know a real fine place. And maybe later, we could go to a dogfight. I heard there's one over—"

"Don't want another woman," Ernest said. "I want her. She's my woman." He tossed another drink down and called for another bottle. The bartender reluctantly came over with a fresh one.

Birch ordered a whiskey. The music began. Lulu Mon-

tana began with "Beautiful Dreamer," a slow, sweet song
that made Birch's heart ache. Although the piano was
slightly tinny, Lulu Montana's voice soared like a graceful
bird taking flight. At the end of the song, there was a hush
in the room, then wild clapping, whistling, and boot
stomping as the audience showed its appreciation. She
launched into the next song, keeping her public enthralled
for about half an hour. Meanwhile, Birch forgot about the
miners, he was so intent on listening to the songbird.

At the finish of "Sweet Betsy from Pike," Lulu Montana
stepped down from a small platform that her skirts had
kept hidden from view during her performance. She
headed for a door near the back when Ernest came stumb-
ling after and caught hold of her arm.

"Sing us some more," he slurred. "I want to buy you a
drink."

She turned and twisted in his drunken grip. "Please let
go of me," she said.

"What do you want? Whiskey?" Ernest drew out a fat
pouch full of gold dust. "Wine. You prob'ly drink wine."
He turned and called out, "Barten', give the little lady a
glass o' wine. Best you have."

Lulu continued to try to pull away. Birch looked over at
the miner, then at his companions. Both had passed out,
Mort having slid off of his chair onto the floor. The young
miner was spread out over the table, his arm cradling an
empty whiskey bottle. The bartender was taking something out from underneath the counter, but Ernest was
faster, drawing his gun with a speed that was astonishing
for a drunken old miner.

"Keep the shotgun where it belongs and get me a bottle
of wine, dammit," he shouted. The voices of the other
patrons slowly hushed, one by one, as they turned to watch
the drama going on at the back of the saloon. The tiny
singer continued to struggle in the miner's grip.

"Now I got me a woman and I want me a bottle of wine," Ernest called out. He seemed to relish the attention.

"I am not your woman," Lulu snapped. "Now let go of me or I'll—" She was never able to finish that threat. A movement to the miner's right made him whip around and fire. The piano player went down, a derringer dropping from his hand. He lay on the floor, clutching his leg and howling in pain and surprise.

Birch had set his drink down by this time and slowly slipped his Navy Colt out of the holster. He took advantage of the confusion and panic caused by the downed piano player and slipped out of sight behind the miner. The bartender, catching Birch's action out of the corner of his eye, brought out a bottle and held it up.

"Here's the best wine in the house," he said in a false hearty voice. "Go enjoy it. Miss Montana, you can take the rest of the night off."

"Ron, please, get the marshal or something. I don't want a night off," she pleaded. "I want this big drunk oaf to let go of me." She hit out ineffectually, pushing away as best she could. Birch admired her spirit. She wasn't intimidated by the intoxicated miner.

Birch cocked his gun in the miner's ear. "Let go of the lady," he ordered in a pleasant tone. "And while you're at it, drop your gun."

The miner was too far gone to understand. "Oh, so you want her for yerself, eh?"

"No, I don't want her for myself," Birch replied reasonably.

"Well, then, mind yer own business and get that gun out of my ear."

It had never occurred to Birch that he might have to shoot him. He knew the miner was just too drunk to be reasonable and not drunk enough to sleep it off until morning.

"Okay, I've had my eye on her all evening," Birch

agreed. It was half the truth. She was an attractive woman. Too attractive for a big ugly man like Ernest the miner.

"Well, then," the drunk said cheerfully, "you'll have to fight me for her." He put his gun in his holster and pulled a chair around for Lulu to sit in. "There you are, little lady," he said in a gallant voice. "You stay there and I'll be back for you in a while." He took off his holster and set it carefully on the table where his friends were passed out.

Birch took off his gun belt and his broadcloth coat as well, placing them both on a nearby chair. The rest of the saloon patrons began to cheer. This is going to be too easy, Birch thought smugly. The miner was already in his cups, and with just one or two well-placed punches, he could put Ernest into dreamland. He looked over at Lulu. Her luminous eyes watched him with—what? Admiration? He couldn't quite tell, but she sure was pretty.

The first punch caught Birch while he was trying to figure out if Lulu's eyes really were green. It sent him flying across a table, the customers scattering to make room, and he landed hard on his right shoulder. When he looked up, Ernest was coming after him, a great grin on his face. A quick glance at Lulu, who looked worried, and he was on his feet, head bent. He butted his head into Ernest's gut, doubling him over, then sent a right upper cut to the miner's chin. Ernest staggered back, groaning.

Birch thought the fight was over, but Ernest suddenly straightened up and with a yell came after Birch. When they grappled, Birch suddenly realized how dangerous this miner was. Underneath the dusty, baggy clothes he wore to mine gold were powerful arms.

Birch and his opponent butted heads, stunning Birch long enough to send them both to the floor. The miner was on top, and Birch received several blows to the head before he got a knee to the stomach. He'd already figured out that this was the miner's weak point, and he kept punching until the drunken miner's eyes glazed over and he finally toppled over like a fallen tree.

Breathing hard, Birch launched himself into the nearest chair and pushed the hair out of his eyes. Everything looked fuzzy and there was a buzzing in his ears. Someone pushed a drink into his hand, and Birch downed it in one gulp, then swiped his shirtsleeve across his sweaty brow. Gradually, the noise in his ears stopped and his vision cleared. Looking around to see how much damage had been done, he noticed that the drunken miner had been dragged out of the premises, along with his companions.

Several of the saloon patrons were gathered round the piano. The piano player had apparently been carted off to get his leg attended to, but someone was plunking away at the keys while they attempted to sing "The Dying Cowboy."

"Another drink for the stranger over there," Birch heard someone shout. As he looked around, he noticed, with some surprise, Cyrus Dundee at a table in the corner, one empty bottle on its side and one half full. Dundee caught Birch looking at him and raised his glass in a toast. Dundee had given Birch the impression that he was too meek to venture out to such a place. Sometimes impressions can be wrong, Birch thought. He raised his glass to Dundee with a friendly nod.

The bartender brought an entire bottle to the table and poured Birch a drink. "On the house," he said, beaming.

Lulu Montana finally approached, gazing gratefully at him. "I want to thank you for standing up for me. You were very brave."

Birch found his voice. "If it hadn't been me, someone would have fought for you. But I was honored to save so sweet a voice."

She smiled and looked at an empty chair next to him. Beneath lowered lashes, she looked at him and asked, "May I?"

Birch roused himself and pulled the chair out for her. "I apologize. I'm forgetting my manners."

As she sat down, Lulu laughed. "They'll come back to you bit by bit. You took some heavy blows to the head." She suddenly leaned forward, a concerned look on her fair face, and asked in a coquettish manner, "Are you sure you're feeling all right? For instance, do you remember your own name?"

Birch laughed. "I suppose you're entitled to know the name of the man who fought for you. My name is Jefferson Birch."

She looked pensive, turning his name around on her tongue. "Birch. That's a nice strong name. I don't suppose I have to introduce myself to you at this point." Birch listened with pleasure to her laughter. It was melodic like her singing. He noticed that she had an empty glass with her. His own drink was still untouched.

"May I pour you a drink?" he asked, looking at the label on the bottle that the bartender had left on his table. It wasn't cheap whiskey this time, it was a bottle of good brandy. "Would you like some brandy?"

She nodded and held out her glass. He poured, his hand shaking just a little.

"You'll be able to get home all right, won't you?" she asked.

"I'll be able to get back to the hotel, if that's what you mean," he assured her. "That miner was a lot tougher than I'd originally thought," he added as an afterthought.

"Oh, you're not from around here," Lulu replied, looking a little surprised. "Where do you come from?"

"Originally from Texas," Birch replied. "I don't have a place I call home, but tomorrow I'll be going back to Grass Valley."

"Grass Valley," she said thoughtfully. "What kind of work do you do?"

Birch didn't feel comfortable enough to tell her the

whole truth. "I'm working for someone in San Francisco," he replied, which was the truth; Arthur Tisdale did have an office there, and Birch was actually working for him. He figured Lulu would draw her own conclusions. Unfortunately, Cyrus Dundee chose that moment to totter over. Birch stood up so abruptly that Lulu gave him a quizzical look. He smiled at her in a reassuring manner and, gesturing to Dundee, who was still making his way over to them, explained, "Someone I don't think you want to know. Excuse me for a moment." He met the bank clerk halfway.

"Mr. Birch, I jusht wanted to tell you that I hope you find the crooked varmints who shtole Mr. Rhodes's money and killed Joe. I hope I was shome help to you thish afternoon."

Birch took Dundee firmly by the elbow. "You did the best you could. Now I think it's about time you went home, Cyrus, while you can still stand."

Dundee straightened up with as much dignity as a drunk could have. "I am fine, Mr. Birch," he said, trying to sound sober. "I know that you want some time alone with your new lady friend and I will leave now." Dundee turned toward Lulu, who had been watching them from a distance, and bowed. She raised her eyebrows in response. The little drunken bank clerk straightened up too fast and staggered back a couple of steps as a result. Then he turned and lurched back to his table.

Birch returned to his table and Lulu, whose green eyes were twinkling with amusement. "What was that all about?"

"He wanted to thank me for something," Birch said, being deliberately vague. He changed the subject. "When I was in Grass Valley yesterday, I saw a poster with your name on it."

"Yes, I'll be performing at Duffy's tomorrow night and maybe for the whole week, if I draw enough of an audience."

"I don't see any problem there," Birch replied. "You have a beautiful voice."

"Thank you," she said, blushing. "This saloon just has a small platform to stand on, but Duffy's in Grass Valley has a real stage." Lulu hesitated before asking shyly, "Will you come to Duffy's tomorrow night?"

"What time do you begin singing?" Birch asked, a half-smile on his face.

"Nine o'clock," Lulu said firmly, brushing his hand with her fingertips. Her touch was soft and warm. As she leaned closer, sweet lilacs scented the air around him.

Birch raised his eyebrows in wonder. "Isn't the man supposed to court the woman?"

Lulu laughed again and replied, "Not if he so gallantly defended her honor and, in doing so, his brains became too addled to ask. Besides, I would like to see more of Grass Valley than just the saloons, and a woman needs an escort to go anywhere besides the general store. Since you became my protector tonight, how can you refuse?"

Birch nodded. How could he indeed?

CHAPTER 8

LULU watched Jefferson Birch leave the saloon. He was the first man who had interested her in a long time. Tall, ruggedly handsome with a touch of humor in his face, he seemed to be a very determined man. But there was something about him that bothered her. She couldn't define it, but she had the definite feeling that he was being reticent about the kind of work he did. He had told her that he was working for someone in San Francisco. Her mind ran through the possibilities. Maybe Birch was a cattle buyer or a land man, but he would have been more open about the former, and he would have been better dressed if he were the latter.

Lulu wondered if Birch might be an outlaw. She had heard of large organized gangs of outlaws who worked adjoining territories with the base being in a large centrally located city like San Francisco. She shook her head at the thought. Whatever Birch was, she wanted to get to know him better.

She was ready to go up to her room when she remembered the funny little man who had come over to talk to Birch. He didn't look like an outlaw who could rob a bank or a train. If he had talked to Birch, he would know more about the man than Lulu had been able to find out all evening.

Her gaze swept the room and came to rest on a passed-out figure at a table in the corner. With determination in every step, Lulu Montana crossed the room and sat down at the table. As if sensing her presence, he raised his head and stared at her through bloodshot eyes, then gazed at the empty bottle on his table.

He reached out a hand and touched her arm. "Just had to make sure you're real," he finally said with a grin that verged on a leer.

Lulu came right to the point. "You were talking to a man I was sitting with earlier this evening."

"Mr. Birsh." The little man had trouble pronouncing Birch's name in his inebriated condition. "A fine man. Upstanding. Keen wits."

"Yes," she replied, then asked, "what was it that you two talked about?"

The man widened his eyes, as if trying to focus them on her. "You sure are pretty. The name's Cyrus Dundee," he said, sticking his hand out.

She shook his hand quickly. Although Lulu performed in saloons, she tried to avoid the men who got as intoxicated as this man, Cyrus Dundee. Forcing a smile, she said, "Thank you for the compliment, Mr. Dundee." Then she tried again. "Could you tell me what you talked about earlier with Mr. Birch?"

"Oh, I can't do that. He'd prob'ly want it kept con—confi—secret." Dundee put a finger up to his lips.

Lulu smiled. She was determined to find out why Birch had come to Nevada City and why he was in Grass Valley. She didn't know why this was so important, she only knew that the images she conjured up about Birch bothered her and she could not let it go.

"I understand. We both know what important work he does," she said in her sweetest voice and watched with satisfaction as Cyrus Dundee nodded. Lulu continued, "Would you like something to drink, Cyrus?"

"Oh," he hiccupped, "I don' think it would be such a good idea. I should go home." He started to get up, but she caught his sleeve.

"You wouldn't want a lady to drink alone, would you?" she asked softly, lowering her eyelashes.

Cyrus sat down and Lulu signaled to the bartender to bring two drinks to her table. When the drinks arrived, Cyrus Dundee looked dubiously at his glass. Lulu picked up her tumbler and said, "Let's have a toast."

He happily agreed, lifting his whiskey unsteadily. "What shall we drink to?"

"To Birch's health," she said, taking a sip.

"Birch's health?" Dundee asked. He shrugged and downed his drink. Lulu motioned to the bartender again to bring the whole bottle. She poured him another one.

"Why drink to Mr. Birch's health?" Dundee asked.

Lulu thought quickly. "Because his work is dangerous."

"It is?" Dundee eyed her doubtfully.

"Well, wouldn't you say that what he does is risky?"

Dundee looked thoughtful. "I guess it is. It could be, if he ever catches up to the outlaws."

"What outlaws?"

"The ones that robbed the bank." Dundee's chest puffed out as he explained, "We think it was the Shirleys. Ever heard of them?" He had put special emphasis on "we."

"The name sounds familiar," Lulu said gravely. "How do you know it was the Shirleys?"

"Because I was there when they robbed the bank," Dundee hiccupped. "I saw 'em plain as day."

Lulu leaned forward, her emerald eyes sparkling. "What did they look like? I've never met anyone who has ever seen an outlaw gang."

For the next five minutes, she listened with rapt interest to the drunk little man's description of the bank robbers. When he was finished, Lulu murmured, "You must be very brave to have endured such an experience."

Dundee perked up. "It was nothing. I did what I had to do." He looked at her slyly and said, "Want to go upstairs? I have some money."

Her first instinct was to slap him. Although she sang in saloons, she wasn't a whore. Some men couldn't make the distinction. However, she kept her temper in check. Cyrus Dundee had given her some valuable information about Birch. Instead, she patted his hand kindly and replied, "I'm not that kind of woman."

He narrowed his bloodshot eyes and asked, "Then why you askin' me all those questions." He had a wounded look on his face, which quickly turned to suspicion. "You must of had a reason for askin' me."

She felt a pang. Since she had turned down his offer of money to take him into her bed, Dundee might begin to think that she had asked all those questions because she had an unusual interest in the bank robbery. But instead, Dundee cracked a smile and said, "Yeah, I should have seen it right from the beginning. You're sweet on Mr. Birch. No wonder you was askin' about him."

Filled with relief, Lulu blushed. Dundee cackled. "I knew he'd fought over you early tonight, but I guess I didn't see that you really liked him. A woman likes to know about a man and his intentions before—" He took another swig of liquor. His face suddenly went slack and his head hit the table. Lulu watched the little man for another minute, but he was out cold.

As she walked up to her room, she pondered what she knew. So, Jefferson Birch was an investigator. That made sense, she thought: he had struck her as an honorable man. Now she knew he was in Nevada City investigating the bank robbery. But why did he have to go to Grass Valley? Was there some connection?

She would see Birch again tomorrow night. Maybe she could find out more from him then.

CHAPTER 9

BIRCH's fight the other night made his ride back to Grass Valley a little uncomfortable. Some of the injuries he had sustained weren't apparent until he woke up in the morning and tried to move. His ribs hurt, one shoulder felt like it had been torn almost out of its socket, an eye and one side of his mouth were swollen, and his nose was tender to the touch.

Birch smiled as his mind's eye conjured up the image of Lulu Montana. It had turned out that they had quite a bit in common. Both of them had traveled extensively and were able to talk about towns and territories that they had both passed through. Toward the end of the evening, she had gotten Birch to reveal that he had been a Texas Ranger. Lulu must have sensed, from the way he had told her, that something unpleasant was attached to his memories of being a Ranger because she had tactfully changed the subject.

Riding back to Grass Valley, Birch felt almost lighthearted as he recounted the evening. It was the first time a woman had not dimmed in comparison to the memory of his wife. Physically, nothing about Lulu reminded him of Audrey, yet she had a sweet nature just like his wife.

When Birch stepped into the sheriff's office, Martin had just put his hat on, ready to go out. He saw Birch and grinned. "Must have been quite a fight last night."

Birch lifted his hand to his still puffy eye, a sheepish grin spreading across his face. "It wasn't in the line of duty. I was defending a lady's honor."

Sheriff Martin chuckled. "I'd say that qualifies. I was just about to go home for supper. Why don't you come along. Elizabeth usually cooks more food than I can eat."

They walked back to a modest two-story house a few blocks behind the jail. A white picket fence ran around a large plot of land. Red and white flowers bloomed along the border of the fence. The aroma of lamb stew wafted through the open windows, and a woman in a calico dress and starched white apron opened the door. She was a pleasant round-faced woman who would have been considered plain if it weren't for her bright smile and rich chestnut hair.

"I see you've brought someone home," she said with a mock frown. Her twinkling eyes gave her good nature away.

"Birch, this is my wife, Elizabeth," the sheriff said by way of introduction.

"It looks as if you've had a bit of a disagreement," Elizabeth said as she stood aside to let them in.

Birch grinned despite his split lip as the sheriff explained, "He's working with me, Libby. Last night he fought to defend a lady's honor."

She inspected Birch doubtfully before asking, "Did you win?"

Both men looked at each other and chuckled.

The inside was as comfortable as the outside was cheery. As they stood in the entry, Birch looked to his left and noted the living room. Two overstuffed chairs flanked a stone fireplace; a large braided rug covered the floor of the hearth.

He followed the sheriff's wife down the hall and to the right into their dining room. A steaming cauldron sat on a large iron trivet in the middle of the table and two places were set.

"Please sit." Elizabeth indicated the two places, explaining, "I have to get the bread out of the oven." Then she bustled through a door into what Birch supposed was the kitchen. She was back in a minute, laden with a tray on which a large round crusty loaf sat with another place setting for herself.

The stew was fragrant with spices and the bread hot and chewy. When all three had finished and Elizabeth was clearing the table, the sheriff indicated that they get up from the table and go into the living area. As they sat in the two comfortable chairs by the fireplace, Elizabeth came in with two bourbons.

"That was a wonderful meal, Mrs. Martin," Birch said.

She smiled with pleasure. "Thank you, Mr. Birch. You're always welcome to come back for a meal."

Martin grinned as she left the room and said in a low voice, "She doesn't always take to the company I bring home."

Birch took a sip of bourbon and replied, "Then I feel honored. You're very lucky to have someone like her." He felt a twinge of jealousy. Chet Martin had everything that Birch wanted: a home, a loving wife, and contentment, something that Birch hadn't known ever since he left Texas.

They sat and drank their liquor in silence. When they had drained their glasses, Birch made a report of his trip to Nevada City. When he was finished, Sheriff Martin nodded. "Doesn't sound like you had much luck. All of that's in the report Marshal McManus sent to me a couple of weeks ago."

Birch had to agree with Martin on that point.

"However," Martin continued, "the notion that information on when the payroll is shipped is somehow getting to the Shirleys could turn out to be a lead for you to follow. I wired some of the other banks that were robbed last year and got back some interesting information. Three of the five banks I contacted had been robbed during a time when the bank had a large payroll in its safe. All three banks have definitely identified the Shirleys as the robbers."

"What about the other two banks?" Birch asked.

"The robbers were caught, and they definitely weren't the Shirley gang."

Birch nodded.

The sheriff shifted in his chair and asked, "Is your partner coming in today?"

"Tomorrow," Birch corrected.

"I guess there isn't much you can do until then."

"I have a few wires to send out," was all Birch would reveal. He took his leave soon after, thanking Elizabeth Martin for the meal and shaking the sheriff's hand once more.

"Bring your partner over to meet me after you meet the stage," he suggested to Birch.

Birch agreed, touched the brim of his hat, and left.

That night, Birch went to see Lulu's performance. Duffy's dance hall had a better reputation than most of the hurdy-gurdies. For one thing, the girls who worked at Duffy's made their living almost solely from dancing with the customers. At less honorable places, many of these women were forced into prostitution.

On the other hand, most of the women at Duffy's were big-boned farm girls with ruddy complexions and calloused hands. But unlike their more unfortunate counterparts who were scantily clad in cheap flimsy gowns or, as Birch discovered in one place, their bloomers, the girls who worked for Duffy's wore dresses that were more appropriate for going to church on Sunday than for a night of boot-stomping fun with strangers. Every once in a while, Birch would notice a hat, ornately decorated with feathers and ribbons, perched upon coarse yellow or brown hair.

Three fiddlers sat in chairs in a corner of the saloon, tuning up. Birch looked around for Lulu, but she didn't appear to be out in the saloon area. Compared to the other women, she would stand out like a shining star. A Chinese girl sidled up to him. She was prettier than most of the other women, her strikingly dark almond-shaped eyes were filled with good humor, and her oval face was framed by smooth black hair. She wore a light blue organdy gown that was much more appropriate than the dark wool and cotton skirts and starched white shirtwaists that most of the women were dressed in.

"Dance?" she asked, holding an ivory silk fan up to her face. She fluttered her lashes at him. The musicians had begun playing a schottische.

He was just about to turn her down when a shiny clean miner came up and grabbed her hand. Most miners don't bother to wash more than once a month. But when they were going to a place like Duffy's, they scrubbed themselves until their skin was raw and put on their Sunday go-to-meeting suit. Birch had never seen so much bear's grease slicking down so much hair in one place.

The dancing girl looked back at Birch and shrugged, then turned back to her partner, and off they whirled into the dancing fray. Birch went up to the bar and ordered a whiskey. He was approached several times by different hurdy girls, then eyed from a distance by those who had been turned down. The bartender was starting to look at him askance when Lulu finally came up to him.

Birch felt a smile spread across his face. She was wearing a pale yellow dress with a cameo at her throat. Her hair was piled up like the night before, dark wisps straying artfully, gold tassels in place.

"You look very nice tonight," he said. "Did you have a good journey here?" Out of the corner of his eye, Birch could see men and women turning to stare at them. And why not? He was there with the most beautiful woman in the place, probably the most beautiful woman in Grass Valley.

Lulu nodded and smiled with her full lips, her green eyes glittering. "Thank you. I hope you're not too sore from the other night."

"Can I buy you a drink?"

She laughed and said, "We're supposed to dance first. Then I get you to buy me a very expensive drink."

The band began playing another schottische. "What are we waiting for?" Birch replied, holding out his hand.

Lulu looked up at him. The lamplight did interesting things to her features. He could almost believe that her face glowed.

The evening passed fast. Lulu was called upon to sing during lulls in dancing. She was received with much enthusiasm by the customers, and soon people were calling out requests. Birch was proud to be seen with her. As the evening wore on, Birch noticed a short, fat man standing in a corner, watching the two of them. This wasn't unusual because Lulu was a beauty, but he turned out to be the saloon owner, Duffy. Finally, he came up to them and asked to speak to Lulu alone. Birch could see their angry gestures from across the room. He was about to go over and find out what the problem was when Lulu returned, two high spots of color on her cheeks. He didn't need to ask her what had happened; she was more than happy to share it with him.

"Duffy seems to think I should be dancing with the other customers," Lulu said tartly. "I reminded him that I was not one of his fandango girls, someone he could order around. I was hired to sing. If I felt like it, I would dance with some of the customers when I wasn't on the stage."

"I hope this hasn't affected your chances of an extended engagement," Birch replied. He was concerned that Lulu might have lost work arguing with the owner over spending all her time with him.

"He's a tyrant," Lulu said, looking unconcerned. With a

wave of her hand, she added, "Tomorrow is my last night here, though."

She caught Birch's stricken expression. Then Lulu laughed softly, leaning over, to brush his jawline with her fingertips. Birch felt his skin tingle where she had touched him.

"Don't worry about me," Lulu admonished. "The smaller mining towns around the area are always hungry for entertainment. I can just take my pick. By Monday night, I'll have drunken miners throwing gold nuggets at my feet while I sing." She tugged at his sleeve, and he took her into his arms just as the band played a waltz.

"I wish this evening would never end," she murmured into his ear.

Birch responded by holding Lulu closer to him. The heady mixture of her perfume and the seductive swaying of the waltz as they whirled around the room in each other's arms were making him dizzy.

When the music ended, they sat down at a table to catch their breath. Birch got up and brought drinks back from the bar.

As she raised her glass to her lips, Lulu looked at him over the rim of her glass and said, "This is the last one for me."

Birch looked around. The saloon crowd was starting to thin out. The evening was coming to a close.

"Where are you staying tonight?" he asked.

"At a boarding house nearby. I think I'm about ready to leave." She took another sip of her drink and stood up. "Would you walk me back to my room?"

Birch nodded, drained his glass, and they left. When they stepped out of the dank, smoky saloon, Birch inhaled the sharp scent of cold, clear night air. A full moon hung like a bright white globe above Grass Valley. Lulu slipped her hand through Birch's arm, and together, they walked slowly down the main street.

Finally, Birch broke the silence. "You haven't told me much about yourself."

"What do you want to know?"

"Where you're from, do you have any family, were you ever married. Things like that."

Her arms were crossed in front of her to keep out the chill. He took off his coat and placed it gently on her white shoulders.

"I moved west a few years ago," she said, "and my family is all gone. I'm alone in this world."

"How did you become a singer?" he asked.

Lulu shrugged and looked down at the ground. "I always had a good singing voice. I was always called upon to sing at church. When I came out to California, I was desperate for work so I answered an advertisement in a newspaper for pretty waiter girls. When I talked to the saloon owner, it became clear to me that a pretty waiter girl was nothing more than another name for prostitute." She wrinkled her nose and laughed. "I was so innocent that I didn't know it until one of the girls served the owner a beer. She was wearing this pretty ostrich feather hat and a lovely little velvet jacket." Lulu fell silent.

Birch prompted her. "But what made you realize the owner was hiring prostitutes?"

He could see her blushing in the moonlight. "That was all she was wearing." There was a pause, then they looked at each other and laughed.

"And you hadn't noticed her manner of dress before this?" Birch asked, still chuckling.

She shook her head. "I had seen the girls only from the waist up from a distance, but didn't get a good look until that moment." Laughing, she added, "You should have seen my face. I think the saloon owner was amused by my reaction. I tried so hard to look unconcerned, which made my shock all the more obvious."

Lulu sighed before continuing. "When it was clear that

I wouldn't work for him under those conditions, he was kind enough to recommend me to a friend who ran a saloon on the other side of town. I was hired to sing, and when it was discovered that people came to hear me, my employer kept me there until the crowd slacked off. By then, other saloons had heard about me and I was able to choose where I worked and under what conditions."

They reached a large house with a sign that announced it was a boarding house. An oil lamp burned in one of the windows. Birch thought he detected a lace curtain moving.

Lulu had turned to face him. She noticed his stare and turned to look in the direction of the house. Smiling, she replied, "That's Mrs. Owen. She fusses over me every time I come back to Grass Valley."

He looked into her green, green eyes. "It must be nice to have someone to fuss over you." His hands on her shoulders, he pulled her to him and they kissed. Her lips were inviting, her arms held on to him, and they stood there for a few more minutes, holding each other. Finally, reluctantly, Lulu pulled away, slipped his coat off her shoulders, and handed it to him.

"Thank you," Lulu said softly, a smile on the lips Birch had just kissed.

"Will I see you again, or was this just a thank you for coming to your rescue the other night?" he asked.

"No," she said quickly. "I'd like to see you again. But I'll be leaving Grass Valley on Sunday."

"There's always Saturday," he replied.

She hesitated for an instant, then said, "Fine."

The unwanted thought flashed through Birch's mind that Swede would be arriving tomorrow morning some-time. Reluctantly, his duty to his job won out. He thought he detected relief in her eyes when he said, "I have to meet a friend tomorrow."

Lulu cocked her head. He could see the frank curiosity in her eyes. "A friend?" she asked.

"He's here to help me. It can't be postponed. Would you be free for dinner tomorrow night?"

She nodded. "It would have to be an early dinner. I begin at the same time as tonight."

He kissed her one more time before watching her let herself into the boarding house. This time, he was certain the lace curtain twitched before he turned away. There were a lot of things on Birch's mind as he walked back to his hotel. He was bothered by how drawn he was to Lulu Montana. She was a beautiful woman, Birch observed. Why shouldn't he be attracted to her? He wondered if part of the reason for his restraint was a feeling of guilt. He'd been with a few women since his wife's death, but this was different. How could he love another woman after Audrey?

CHAPTER 10

OLE "Swede" Tronsgaord was relieved when the stagecoach pulled up to the Wells Fargo station in Grass Valley. The two-day journey on the Southern Pacific Railroad had been relaxing compared to the one day by stagecoach. Swede had endured not only the spine-jogging pace but also the close quarters with three other passengers.

Two of his chance companions, a schoolteacher and a young woman traveling to Grass Valley to meet her intended husband and his family, were acceptable, even pleasant. But the fourth passenger was a pudgy, sweaty, traveling salesman in a bowler. If his body odor didn't offend everyone in the tight quarters, his incessant chatter about something called "insurance" caused Swede and the other travelers to shrink from him. This insurance salesman made the one-day trip seem like a week to Swede, who vowed that when it was time to go home, he would make sure that there were no other insurance salesmen on his stagecoach.

The sun beat down, washing everything in a dazzling white. When Swede gratefully stepped off the stagecoach, he glimpsed a mountain range in the distance. The town was surrounded by low green hills. Grass Valley was a large town, probably one of the largest towns Swede had seen since his visit to San Francisco a year ago. It had been three years since he had left Norway, promising his beloved wife, Greta, that he would send for her when he had saved enough money for her passage.

Waiting the three more months it took for Greta to come by ship and land was nothing for him. In fact, he had been nervous about seeing her again. What if her feelings for him had changed? What if the same was true for him? But when she stepped off the train in San Francisco, Swede knew he had been worrying for nothing. Sometimes he woke up and watched his now pregnant wife sleeping contentedly by his side. It seemed as if those three years apart had never happened.

Swede's thoughts turned to Jefferson Birch. He was certainly grateful to the ex-Texas Ranger for his current job as town marshal. Before he'd met Birch, he had been working in a logging camp. It was not steady work, and certainly a dangerous job. Not that being a lawman didn't have its dangers. But the dangers came from men, and men were predictable.

There were so many hazards around a logging camp. A log could suddenly work loose from the drag uphill and kill a distracted man who might be standing in its deadly path. Working around two-handed saws could lead to serious injury. He had known plenty of loggers with less than ten fingers.

Swede himself had been the victim of a felled tree. The camp doctor had told him that he would never walk again. When Swede was able to get around on crutches, the foreman had given Swede a job in the mess tent. No one in the camp expected Swede would ever mend properly, but he had proved them all wrong. Now he walked with a slight limp that only those who watched Swede closely could detect.

Trying to shake the ominous feeling that he'd had since receiving Birch's wire, Swede went around to the board-walk to pick up his bag. The bags and boxes that had been stored on top of the stagecoach had been tossed off on the boardwalk by the stagecoach driver. Squinting against the bright day, he searched for his gear. When he couldn't find it, he began to wonder if it had fallen off between

Sacramento and here. As he looked around, he caught sight of his gear at Birch's feet, next to a building.

Swede broke into a grin and went toward him. "Birch, it's good to see you again!"

The man came forward and stuck out his hand. "Same here, Swede."

Swede noticed something different about his friend. All the time Swede had known Birch, there had been a distant sadness to the former Texas Ranger. Swede had always suspected that Birch had a tragic past that was somehow tied up with the Texas Rangers. Any time the subject of the Rangers was broached, Birch became quiet, answering only in one or two words.

Here in Grass Valley, Birch was actually smiling and pumping Swede's arm with enthusiasm instead of his usual reserve.

"Bet you're hungry," Birch said.

Swede's stomach was still bloated from a greasy breakfast of beans and bacon. He had eaten early that morning at a way station while the driver soaked the wooden wheels so they would fit the iron rims snugly for the last leg of the journey. He put his hand to his stomach and shook his head. "I could use a drink, though," he said. "Then I thought we could get to work."

Once inside a nearby saloon, cradling a mug of beer, Swede listened as Birch told him what he'd been doing the past three days. Swede was working his way through a second beer by the time Birch finished his account.

"What do you need me for?" Swede asked.

Birch leaned back in his chair and crossed his arms. "Your tracking abilities." Swede gave his friend a skeptical look. Birch added, "All right. You're also a lawman."

The big Norwegian made a vague gesture and said, "You have a sheriff here in Grass Valley and a marshal in Nevada City."

"That's true, but they're also involved in the delivery of

payrolls. They're indirectly tied to the robberies. Remember Grant's Pass."

How could Swede forget? The marshal had been in cahoots with one of the saloon owners, and together, they led a band of road agents who robbed, and sometimes killed, miners for their gold and relieved the occasional stagecoach of its logging payroll. Birch had been instrumental in bringing the leaders and their band of outlaws to justice.

After leaving the saloon, Birch introduced Swede to the sheriff, Chet Martin.

"So you're the man Birch brought in. If he thinks you're suited for this work, then you must be."

Birch replied, "He's a town marshal up in Oregon. Town by the name of Grant's Pass."

Martin rubbed his chin in thought. "That's near Klamath Falls, right? I got a cousin who lives up there." He turned to the subject at hand. "Can you tell me what your plans are, Birch?"

"I thought we'd explore the hills surrounding this area, become familiar with them. Maybe we can pick up a trail."

The sheriff nodded. "When the bank was robbed, our posse went into the hills and tried to find tracks. We were at it till the sun went down. Never found so much as a broken twig. The Shirleys must be a clever bunch." He was frowning now. "Listen, Birch—I just got some information that the Shirleys have been spotted around the mining camps north of here. You might be better off heading up there. They do show up in mining camps and small towns from time to time when they want to spend some of the money they've stolen."

"So people have spotted them before?" Swede asked. "Why didn't they arrest them?"

" 'Cause the Shirleys are a dangerous bunch. A lot of men don't have the courage or the determination to catch 'em," Martin explained, then added, "and most of the witnesses were drunk at the time. They were in no condition to arrest a bunch of outlaws."

After Swede was sworn in as a deputy sheriff, the two men took their leave and headed for the stables. While Birch saddled up Cactus, Swede negotiated with the stable owner for a horse. He ended up with a large reddish bay, commonly called a blood bay.

They rode to the southeast edge of town before Birch called a halt. "This is the way the gang went, according to the sheriff. You'll notice that it's the closest escape route. We passed the bank about half a mile back."

Swede nodded. "I saw it. What time of day did they rob the Grass Valley Bank?"

Birch shifted in his saddle and said, "In the afternoon. Around three o'clock." Cactus stamped the ground and twitched his tail impatiently.

They nudged their horses into action.

"You don't really think we'll find anything up there, do you?" Swede asked doubtfully.

"Not any tracks. It's been over a month since the robbery, and the one in Nevada City was a few weeks ago," Birch replied. "But the sheriff was thoughtful enough to mark the trail that the posse used. We'll follow it as far as it goes, then go a little farther and see if we can find anything useful."

They found the markers with no problem. Sheriff Martin had tied strips of red bandanna along the trail. The strips were now faded from the elements, but still easily seen. The day had turned even hotter, and soon Swede wished for a light breeze to cool the sweat that trickled down the small of his back. He didn't say anything to Birch, but he felt that tramping around the hills outside of Grass Valley was a waste of time. He wondered whether his friend was losing his concentration, allowing small details to distract him. This wasn't the way Jefferson Birch would have acted a few years ago.

Sheriff Martin's suggestion of traveling up north was, to Swede's way of thinking, more practical. And there was merit in the idea that someone was getting information on payroll deposits and passing the information on to the Shirleys. It was the only explanation. Why weren't they looking for people who might be able to get that knowledge? It would mean a trip out of town, checking the log of the railroad companies around the area, but it would be doing a hell of a lot more than wandering out in the hills of Grass Valley, the cruel sun beating down on them.

They stopped once at a river to water the horses and to quench their own thirst. Swede looked up at his friend, who was kneeling by the running water, and on impulse, asked, "Are you all right, Birch?"

The ex-Texas Ranger looked down, the expression on his face obscured by the brim of his hat. "Sure. I'm fine. Why?"

Swede shrugged, suddenly feeling uncomfortable, and replied, "No reason in particular. You just seem different."

To his surprise, Birch let out a hearty laugh and said, "It must show that I've met someone. A woman. Met her just a few days ago."

This was a surprise. Birch had never confided in Swede before.

"A woman," Swede repeated, stunned. "You've met a woman?"

Birch looked at Swede, an unreadable expression on his face, then stood up, jamming his hat back on his head. "Her name's Lulu Montana. She's singing in a saloon here in town. You'll meet her tonight."

As they forded the river and continued to follow the trail, Swede guessed that Lulu Montana was the reason Birch didn't want to go too far from town today. But he also couldn't get rid of that bad feeling he'd had ever since deciding to join Birch in tracking down the Shirleys.

CHAPTER 11

THE trip into the hills was a disappointment. Birch had been hoping to find something, a place where outlaws might have holed up, something, anything. Instead, the two men, feeling tired and dusty, rode back into Grass Valley before dusk.

Birch met Lulu for an early dinner, then straight over to Duffy's Dance Hall. Swede was already there. The meeting was not the success that Birch had imagined it would be. As he introduced them, he thought he detected a wary look in Swede's eyes. It appeared to Birch as though, upon meeting Swede, Lulu pulled back just a bit.

The three of them sat and talked for a while, Birch and Swede going through three and four beers respectively. Birch noticed that he and Lulu did most of the talking.

Lulu must have noticed, too. "What is it you do exactly, Swede?" she asked, cocking her head slightly to one side to show interest.

"I'm a town marshal up north," was his curt reply.

"Grass Valley must be out of your territory."

"It is," he said, nodding shortly.

Birch explained, "He's working with me for a few weeks." Out of the corner of his eye, he saw Swede staring at Lulu, but when he turned his head, Swede lowered his eyes to his half-empty mug.

There was an uncomfortable silence. Then Lulu leaned forward and said to Birch, "So, tell me what you did today." The musicians started playing before Birch could answer, and Lulu stood up. "Well, gentlemen. I must go," she said, turning to Swede and adding, "it was nice to meet you." With a meaningful look at Birch, she walked to the stage and began to sing.

"She has a nice voice," Swede said before draining his mug.

Birch watched his friend for a moment, then said, "Yes, she does."

They sat there and listened. At the end of her song, Swede got up. "I have got to get some sleep now. It's been a long day. I'll see you in the morning."

Birch stayed until the saloon closed.

"I don't think your friend likes me much," Lulu said lightly as they began their slow walk back to her boarding house.

Birch sighed. "He's just very tired. He spent the last three days on a train and a stagecoach. Then we immediately started to do what we came here to do."

"What exactly is it that you're doing here, Birch?" she asked. Taking his arm and leaning against him, Lulu added, "I know I shouldn't ask something like that, but I'm curious. I've known you for three days, and I think I'm entitled to know a little more about the man I'm seeing."

Birch smiled. "I guess it's really no secret. I'm just not used to talking about my work." He told her about the bank robberies and the Shirley gang.

Lulu sighed, her elegant face tilting up to see the stars. She stopped and faced him, taking his hand. "I've read about the gang. I just hope you're careful."

Birch chuckled. "I've been careful up until now. I don't intend to change." They kissed, then kissed again. While he held her close, he asked if she could stay another day.

"I'll be going to Emigrant Gap tomorrow to sing for the miners."

"That's not too far, is it?" Birch asked. He'd hoped that she would find work in another saloon here in Grass Valley.

"It's just north of Nevada City," she said. After a slight hesitation, she added, "That's where one of the robberies took place, isn't it?" Lulu didn't wait for an answer. Instead, she kissed him long and hard, then pulled away. "You'll come visit me up there, won't you?"

"I'll try," he replied. Birch watched her until she had closed the door of the boarding house. Then he headed back to his hotel, humming the whole way.

CHAPTER 12

SWEDE was troubled by what he had witnessed in the saloon the other night. When he had been introduced to Lulu Montana, he had wanted to like her. There was something very charming about her, but Swede also sensed something brittle inside her as well. He tried to sound enthusiastic for Birch's sake, but his heart wasn't in it.

When they met the next morning, Swede noticed that Birch seemed preoccupied.

"Is something wrong?" he asked.

"No," was Birch's blunt reply.

"What needs to be done today?" Swede asked, trying to ignore his partner's brusqueness.

Birch sighed. He took his hat off and rubbed the back of his head in a pensive manner. "I think we'd better take the sheriff's advice and start making the rounds of the mining towns. Since they've been spotted up north, we'll head that way first."

They got their horses from the stable and, since they didn't know where they would end up come sundown, loaded bedrolls and supplies on the saddles. Swede and Birch rode for an hour in silence.

"Lulu's gone for a few days," Birch said. "She's found work in another town."

"Think you'll ever see her again?" Swede asked.

A short silence, then Birch replied, "Maybe."

Swede sensed that Birch wasn't ready to talk about her yet, so he changed the subject. "Where are we headed?"

"There's a few mining towns up this way that I thought

we'd ride through first. We should be within half an hour of one right now."

Sure enough, they came to a makeshift town called Angels Camp. There was a tent that served as a saloon, one that served as a kitchen, and dozens of miners roaming around between the two.

Birch and Swede dismounted and walked into the kitchen tent. An old-timer, wielding a ladle, was stationed behind a large cooking pot. He squinted at the two strangers who were lining up with the miners for grub.

When Birch got to the front of the line, the old man looked at them distrustfully. "You don't look like no miners who been working on claims in this area."

"We're just passing through," Birch assured him. "We'll be glad to pay you for a meal." He pulled out a coin and passed it to the man.

The old-timer took it, then slopped stew into their bowls and shoved a couple of squares of cornbread at them.

"You seen any more strangers around these parts?" Birch asked.

"I ain't seen no one, mister. No one but you two," he added, pointing the dripping ladle at them. "Now get on through the line. You're holding up these other workin' fellas."

Birch and Swede ate their stew quickly. There was no table. Men stood or squatted if they couldn't find a rock or a tree stump to perch on. A man came up to Birch and Swede. He was probably about twenty years old, razor-thin, and sparse stubble barely covered a pock-marked jaw.

"I heard you fellas talkin' to Cookie back there," he said.

Birch looked at Swede, then back at the kid. He nodded. "That's right. We're looking for a couple of bank robbers. There's talk that they sometimes come into mining camps and small towns when they get bored."

The young fellow nodded eagerly. "I heard about them.

There's a couple of strange types who sometimes show up here on Saturday nights. Can you describe 'em to me?"

Birch gave cursory descriptions, but by the time he was finished, the young man was shaking his head. "Don't sound like anyone I've seen around here, mister. Sorry." He turned and walked away.

"Even if he'd seen 'em," a voice said behind Birch and Swede, "he wouldn't tell you the truth."

They turned around to face a short man with a droopy mustache. "Why not?" Swede asked.

The man shrugged. "We don't know you. Why should we tell you anything?"

Swede laughed and in an aside to Birch, muttered, "Just like a miner."

The miner stepped forward, his hands suddenly becoming fists. "What did you say, stranger?"

Swede turned his attention back to the short man and in an even voice, repeated, "I said, 'Just like a miner.' "

The short man lunged at Swede with no warning, knocking his stew bowl up in the air as he threw a punch at the big Norwegian's jaw. Swede stepped easily to the side and dug his elbow into the man's ribs. The miner staggered a few steps, then regained his footing and turned on Swede again. By this time, several other miners had joined in the fray, taking swings at Birch and at each other.

A gunshot stopped the action as quickly as the insult had started it. Cookie stood in front of his tent, brandishing a shotgun.

"You all have had your fun now. Get back to work." He turned to the two strangers and added, "And you two can just git on your horses and ride on out of here. You caused enough trouble fer one day."

Still breathing hard, the duo stumbled over to their horses. Swede noticed that Birch had a bloody nose and a ripped shirt.

"Hey!" called the short miner.

Ignoring him, Swede and Birch walked faster toward their horses.

"Hey!" He caught up with them. His eye was starting to close and he was limping a little, but he grinned good-naturedly. "Look, no hard feelings, okay? That was the best damned fight I ever started."

"Glad to hear it," Birch replied, trying to stop the blood with a bandanna. They both turned away, ready to mount their horses.

"Wait! You asked about those strangers."

Birch and Swede turned back and waited.

The short miner continued, "I seen 'em around, but not here. Sometimes when I go up to Emigrant Gap, I see 'em at some of the saloons there."

"Thanks," said Swede with a nod.

The trip to Emigrant Gap took no more than half an hour. The mining town was larger than Angels Camp, a combination of tents, makeshift buildings, and permanent structures. The place was almost deserted in the middle of the day. Most of the residents had gone off to their stakes to find nuggets and dust. There were a few women and children, and some older folks. Swede and Birch approached one of the larger structures, a general supply store.

"What can I do for you boys?" asked a stout sharp-faced woman as she emerged from a back room. She wore a grimy apron, on which she was wiping her hands.

Birch bought a box of bullets. Swede walked around and looked at all the mining and food supplies that were available for the folks at Emigrant Gap.

"You boys just passing through?" the woman asked. Swede noticed for the first time that she was slightly cross-eyed.

"We may stop here for the night," Birch replied.

"There's gonna be some entertainment tonight at the

big saloon on the edge of town. A singer. She just came into town this morning."

When they left the general store, Swede turned to Birch. "Why didn't you ask that woman back there about the Shirleys?"

Birch looked amused at his friend's bewilderment. "After our last experience, I'd think you'd be a little more cautious."

Swede shrugged, irritated. "She was just an old woman."

"An old woman with her hand on a shotgun that was hidden under the counter," Birch pointed out.

Swede flushed. He hadn't seen any shotgun. While Birch was buying bullets, he'd been wandering around the store.

"That entertainer that the woman mentioned. It's Lulu Montana, right?"

Birch looked down, hunching his shoulders, and pushed his hat back before giving Swede a sideways glance. "Could be," Birch said carefully, squinting straight ahead now into the heart of Emigrant Gap. "We'll go to the saloon tonight. I want to look around and ask questions there after the miners become more social. Heck, maybe the Shirleys will show up and we can bring 'em all back to Grass Valley."

It was about ten o'clock before the saloon started to fill up. Birch and Swede had come in early and were seated at a table near the entrance of the large tent. Tamped earth served as a floor, but a low wooden platform served as a stage at one end of the saloon. Several musicians stood on the stage, plucking their fiddles.

The music started, a reel, and miners started grabbing women to dance with. If a miner couldn't find a woman, he danced with another miner. Birch and Swede sat and drank, watching the dancing with amusement. Occasionally, a miner would step on his partner's foot and the partner's reaction would vary from hopping on his good foot to kicking the offender's shins. After a few dance numbers, the lead fiddler stood up.

"Folks, we got us a treat tonight. A singer named Lulu Montana. She's not askin' for nothin' except what you want to give her. So's if you like what you hear, throw up a nugget or two in appreciation."

Lulu Montana was helped onto the platform. Swede looked over at Birch's face, but there was no expression. He wondered if Birch had known she was here. If not, it was quite a coincidence.

Lulu wore a plain dark skirt and white shirtwaist. Her voice was sweet and clear, holding her audience spellbound as she sang one song after another. When she was done, Lulu gave a quick curtsy. The roar of approval by the miners was only surpassed by the number of gold nuggets and dust that were thrown at Lulu.

With the help of one of the musicians, she gathered up her payment and left the stage. Birch still sat where he was, but his eyes never left Lulu's movements in the crowd.

"Do you want another beer?"

Birch silently handed his mug to his friend, his eyes still following Lulu. Swede went up to the bar. As he started to head back, he noticed Lulu sitting with a miner at a nearby table. He was a broad fellow with greasy black hair and whiskers.

"You sure got a pretty singin' voice, missy," Swede overheard the miner saying.

"Oh, I bet you say that to every singer who comes around here," Lulu laughed.

"Sure don't, little lady. Can I pour you a drink?" He had a bottle of rye at his table and two glasses.

She accepted, and Swede watched her sip the rye daintily. The miner tossed his drink down and poured himself another. Looking closer, Swede could see the bleary look of a man who had already had more than enough drinks.

"Why are you here tonight, spending your hard-earned money on me?" Lulu asked, batting her eyelashes at him.

Swede didn't know where this was going, but he was too

fascinated to leave. He decided to delay going back to the table just a little longer.

Lulu Montana leaned toward the miner, who flushed and replied, "A feller's got to have someone to spend his gold on."

"It must be very dangerous."

"Wha' ish?" he asked, slurring his words.

Lulu gave him a wide-eyed innocent look and said, "Moving all that gold from your claim to a safe place."

"Oh, that can be chancy, all right," the miner agreed.

"I've heard that the road to Nevada City has a band of road agents every five miles. Why, if one of them doesn't get you, the other ones will."

"Oh, I don't go down south with my gold," the miner was quick to say. "My claim is up closer to Sierra City."

"How often do you have to make the trip?"

The miner seemed to need to think about that one. "Well, I got to go there tomorrow. Got a whole load of nuggets to take in to the assay office. Besides, I usually go with a group of others. We watch out for each other." He smiled and patted her hand clumsily. "So don't you worry about me, honey."

Swede had heard enough. He brought the beers back to the table, and after they drained their mugs, the two men left.

When they were outside, Birch stayed quiet. Swede broke the silence. "Why didn't you tell Lulu you were there?"

Birch shrugged. "She seemed to be busy with another fellow."

Swede couldn't swear to it, but he thought he detected some hurt in Birch's tone. Having overheard Lulu's conversation with the miner, Swede was having some unpleasant notions about Lulu, but knowing how Birch felt about her, he decided not to talk about his suspicions.

"I listened in on some of their conversation," Swede confessed.

Birch looked up sharply. "What were they talking about?"

Swede hated to lie, so he told Birch a half-truth. "Mining. She was asking him about his claim." Swede changed the subject. "Did you see anyone who might have looked like a Shirley?"

Birch shook his head and said, "I talked to a few customers while you were getting the beers, but no one seems to remember them."

"The descriptions on the poster could fit any number of men. What shall we do now?"

Birch looked morose. "We could either go back to Grass Valley and start interviewing everyone connected with the payroll deliveries or we can continue wandering around from one camp to another." He gave a weary sigh. "This investigation isn't getting us anywhere."

"For once, I agree with you," Swede replied, clapping Birch on the shoulder. "I suggest that we go back to Grass Valley or Nevada City. There are a few things I'd like to investigate."

Birch looked at Swede, curiosity overcoming his melancholy. "What? Have I missed something?"

The big Norwegian hesitated, then shook his head. "I'll tell you if it's worth anything. For now, let's just leave it alone."

He was going to find out more about Lulu Montana from his contacts. If he was wrong, he didn't want to risk his friendship with Birch. If he was right, he would have a tough decision to make.

CHAPTER 13

BIRCH found it hard to sleep that night. He couldn't stop thinking about Lulu Montana. Whenever he was with her, he felt as if he were under a spell. He could no longer imagine what it would be like never to see Lulu again. Birch drifted off to sleep with thoughts of a future with Lulu Montana in his head.

The next day, Swede and Birch were back in Grass Valley. Swede excused himself and disappeared, and Birch spent the rest of the day going through all the facts on the bank robberies, trying to find common ground. He checked the names of the stagecoach drivers, but unless they were conspiring together, there was no basis for suspecting them because different drivers were used on the stage runs. Birch would check the telegraph operators—one of them might be intercepting messages and passing them on to the Shirleys.

The day wore on slowly for Birch. He knew that Swede had mentioned some investigating that he was doing on his own, and Birch had agreed to give Swede the freedom to launch his own line of questioning. But he was now beginning to feel uneasy about it. Swede didn't show up all day at the sheriff's office, where they were to meet.

It wasn't until the following morning that Swede appeared. Birch was sitting at the deputy's desk when the big Norwegian entered, a paper in his hand and a sheepish expression on his face.

"Where have you been?" Birch asked. "I hope whatever you did yesterday had something to do with the Shirleys. We can't afford to waste time on other pursuits."

Swede cleared his throat and said, "I spent all of yesterday at the telegraph office, sending wires to the Jacksonville sheriff in Oregon. He has a brother who lives in Kentucky, and I was able to get this information on the Shirley gang."

Birch was impressed with the work Swede had done. He stood up, suddenly feeling lighter than he had since entering this investigation. "What do you have?" he asked, trying not to sound too eager.

Swede avoided his eyes and replied, "You're not going to like what I've found. In fact, you may feel like hitting me."

"Well, what is it?" Birch asked impatiently.

"I didn't want to tell you until I'd done some checking on Lulu's background," Swede said reluctantly.

Birch didn't move. He didn't breathe. He didn't even feel shock or surprise, just a profound disappointment. In an unemotional voice, he said, "Tell me."

Swede laid the facts out for Birch. "She's Lulu Montana Shirley," Swede began, consulting his slip of paper. He paused before continuing. "At age seventeen, she married Emmet Shirley, oldest brother of the Shirleys. Two years later, the Shirleys decided to move to California. Her husband, Emmet, died on the trek west. That was four years ago." Swede avoided looking at his friend when he'd finished. He carefully laid the paper on the desk for Birch to pick up and study if he wished.

Birch stared straight ahead, trying to sort everything out. In a cold and controlled voice, he asked, "What made you decide to check Lulu's background?"

Swede related the events of the night before last, explaining Lulu's behavior with the miner at Emigrant Gap. When he was finished, Swede added, "I didn't want to tell you much about her conversation with that miner the night before last until I had a chance to look into her background."

Nodding in resignation, Birch said, "I guess this makes her the best suspect as the Shirleys' informant."

Swede ran a hand through his shaggy white-blond hair and replied, "It appears that way. At the very least, she has a lot of explaining to do."

Birch stood up abruptly, his jaw set. In a sharp tone, he said, "I guess she does, at that."

Swede maintained a studied silence. Birch let out a deep sigh and sat on the edge of the desk, his arms folded tightly across his chest.

"When do you want to start for Emigrant Gap?" Swede asked. When he got no answer, he said, "You have to admit that Lulu's past association with the Shirleys makes her more of a suspect than anyone else so far."

Reluctantly, Birch replied, "We'd better go there now. I don't even know if she'll be there tonight." He picked up his hat, and together, they headed for the stables.

On the ride up there, Birch contemplated what Swede had told him about her and the miner. Even if Lulu Montana was in collusion with the Shirley gang, they robbed banks, not miners, didn't they? Maybe the Shirleys were planning to hold up another bank—a bank that had no large payroll, but that was frequented by miners from around the area. This was a reasonable explanation to Birch, but it didn't leave him satisfied. He still found it hard to believe that Lulu Montana was associated with the Shirleys.

Another thought occurred to him—one that chilled his blood: he had mentioned to Lulu that he was investigating the Shirleys. It stood to reason that she was keeping an eye on Birch by acting interested in him. Had the fight scene at the Nevada City saloon been staged for his benefit? If so, someone in Nevada City was responsible for giving Lulu information on Birch.

Birch ran through the list of people he had talked to in Nevada City and felt that he could eliminate the doctor and the newsman. Both men had nothing to do with the payroll shipment. Rhodes and Dundee, Marshal McManus and Deputy Wells—any of these men could have talked to Lulu. Then Birch remembered seeing Cyrus Dundee at the saloon that night. Lulu had probably seen them talking. Was it possible that she talked to Dundee afterward? The bank clerk had been very drunk, and Birch was willing to bet that she had been able to get him to talk.

Swede and Birch arrived in Emigrant Gap in the late afternoon. Even on a Sunday, the camp was deserted. Birch and Swede dismounted their horses at the saloon tent and went inside. While most of the miners disregarded Sunday as a day of rest when they had a claim to work, a few men were sitting in the saloon, observing the Sabbath by sipping whiskey or rye.

Birch tossed a couple of dollars on the bar and ordered two whiskeys. When the bartender set the glasses in front of them, Birch asked, "Is Lulu Montana still here?"

The bartender shrugged indifferently and started to turn away. Swede clamped a large hand on the man's shoulder and spun him around.

The bartender's face turned pasty, and he raised his hands defensively. "Look, mister. I don't want no trouble, but I don't want to send trouble to the lady."

"We're not here to cause any trouble," Birch said, nodding to Swede, who let go of the bartender's shoulder. "Not for you or for Miss Montana. We just need to speak to her." He flashed his deputy sheriff badge. Rubbing his shoulder, the bartender gave directions to Lulu's lodgings.

Lulu was staying in one of the permanent buildings, a combination hotel and gambling parlor. Birch turned to Swede and said, "I'll go up alone."

Hands in his pockets, Swede nodded and stayed in the gambling parlor.

Birch walked down the hall, hat in hand. When he

knocked, the whole door, a rough-hewn pine, shook in its frame.

Lulu opened the door, her eyes widening in surprise. She looked momentarily flustered before a smile spread across her face. "Birch, how did you find me? This is a pleasant surprise!" She stepped aside to let him in. When he brushed past her, he inhaled the scent of lilacs. The room was bare, except for a straight narrow bed with a lumpy mattress and a small much-used porcelain wash-stand.

Birch heard the door close firmly. He turned around to face her, and a moment later, she was in his arms. "I know it's only been a few days, but I've missed you," she said, her face in his shoulder. She sighed contentedly as Birch awkwardly held her, ashamed to bring up the subject of the Shirleys.

"Lulu," he began gently, taking her by the shoulders and holding her away from him. Her face tilted up toward him, lovely in the late afternoon sun that shone through the one window in the room. "Lulu, I just found out something. Something about you. And I need to know if it's true."

A subtle change in her expression told him all he needed to know.

"I just found out you were once married to Emmet Shirley."

Lulu pulled back from him and turned away, ostensibly to look out the one small window. Her voice was harsh. "I'd rather not talk about it."

Birch started toward her, then stopped and tried again. "The other day, I mentioned the Shirleys and you acted as if you'd only read about them in newspapers. Don't you understand that the fact you hid your association with the Shirleys makes you a suspect in the bank robberies?"

She whirled around to face him, her green eyes flashing, her face twisted in anger. "A suspect, am I? Why? Because

I'm Emmet's widow? Since when could a dead man rob a bank?" She let out a harsh laugh. "I haven't seen his brothers for years."

Birch looked down at his hands. "Lulu, Swede overheard you talking to a miner the night before last." As he related to her what Swede had told him, the color slowly drained from her face.

"So you were there and you didn't even tell me?" Tears formed in Lulu's eyes as she whispered, "I suppose you already suspected me and wanted nothing to do with me."

"Lulu," Birch began, "that was not the reason I didn't approach. I saw you with that miner and I didn't know if—"

Lulu stared at him, comprehension slowly dawning. "Birch," she said softly, coming over and laying a gentle hand on his arm, "he was just a customer who admired my singing. We talked. I asked him about his work, the way I asked you about what you do. It was just conversation. Swede must have misunderstood what was said. That's all."

"Have you had any contact with the Shirley family recently?"

She shook her head. "None."

"Do you have any idea where they might go, where they might live?"

"I'm sorry, Birch. I just don't know."

He looked up at her. "When I mentioned the Shirleys to you that first time, why didn't you tell me?"

She gave him a small bitter smile. "It's not a part of my life that I'm proud of, Birch. If you were me, would you mention that you were once married to a Shirley?"

Birch grinned. "No, I guess not."

They held each other for a few minutes, then Lulu pulled away again and said softly, "But I do have a confession to make."

"What is it?" Birch smiled down at her lovely contrite face.

"When I first met you, that man came up to you in Nevada City, remember?"

He nodded.

"Well, when you left, I was very curious about you, I went by his table and talked to him about you. He told me about the bank robbery, that he had been a witness."

"Why do I have a feeling that there's more to this?"

She hesitated, her hands worrying each other, then she began to pace slowly. "There was a teller killed in that robbery, wasn't there?"

"Yes," Birch said slowly.

"I don't believe that my in-laws robbed that bank," she replied, adding quickly, "maybe they robbed those other banks, but I don't think that they robbed the one in Nevada City."

"Why?"

Lulu cocked her head slightly to the side and continued, "My in-laws would never kill anyone. I'm sure of that."

"Can you tell me why you're so certain about this?"

She frowned, her mouth a crooked line. "I knew the family for a number of years before Emmet and I were married. My guess is that they didn't rob the bank in Nevada City."

"I thought of that, too," Birch said, rubbing the back of his neck. "According to my information, the Shirleys have never so much as hurt anyone, and then, with this robbery, a teller is gunned down in cold blood. Why kill him after he's already opened the safe and they have what they wanted?"

They gazed at each other in silence. Lulu finally took his hand. He moved closer, reaching for her, and she came into his arms willingly.

CHAPTER 14

SWEDE had spent the hour playing monte in the gambling parlor. At the start of the game, he had won quite a lot of money. But by the time Birch came back, Swede was starting to lose badly, and it was a relief to leave the table.

Before he could talk to Birch and find out what information he had gotten from Lulu, he caught sight of her, hair slightly disheveled and a triumphant gleam in her eye, trailing in after Birch.

"Did she tell you anything useful?" Swede asked, pointedly ignoring Lulu.

"Why don't you ask her?" Birch replied mildly. He put his arm around her shoulders and asked her, "Do you mind answering his questions, Lulu?"

With wide green eyes, she looked up at him and said lightly, "Of course not." As she turned her gaze to Swede, he thought her ice-green eyes narrowed just slightly. A cold smile in his direction confirmed his suspicions. "Go ahead. I have nothing to hide."

By the time the interrogation ended, Swede was still not convinced that she hadn't met with the Shirleys in a long time, but he couldn't outright accuse her. It was clear that Birch believed her. Swede doubted the widow of an outlaw could live in the same area as her in-laws and not be in contact with them. She was still Swede's prime suspect.

He noticed that she was also upset, her arms crossed in front of her and her chin determinedly set. As Swede studied her in silence, Lulu turned to Birch, a worried expression on her face. "I don't think Swede believes me, Birch. I don't know what else I can say to convince him."

Birch glanced at Swede, who shrugged.

"Swede is just doing his job," Birch replied in a soothing tone. "You do have a connection to the Shirleys, Lulu, whether you've seen them these past four years or not."

Lulu smiled at Birch. "You're right." She turned to Swede. "If I find out anything, you'll be the first to know."

"Maybe that's true," conceded Swede, "but you must know that they've been seen in this area and you travel around here from town to town."

Swede couldn't rid himself of the notion that Lulu Montana was putting on an act. He didn't like the fact that Birch was starting to fall in love with Lulu and there was still a good chance that she was somehow involved with, and could lead them to, the Shirley gang.

"I'd like a few minutes alone with Lulu," Birch told Swede. "I'll meet you outside, then we'll head back to Grass Valley."

Swede nodded, then glanced at Lulu. "Ma'am," he said, "thank you for answering those questions. It couldn't have been pleasant for you."

She gave him a chilly smile.

On the way back to Grass Valley, Swede asked, "Do you really think Lulu is innocent, Birch?"

"Why would she lie when she knows we can verify her story?" Birch replied.

"How?"

Birch eyed his friend impassively for a moment, then said, "We could check the dates of the towns she's visited with the dates of the robberies."

Swede slapped his forehead. "Of course! Why didn't I think of that?"

Birch nodded shortly. "I'd rather that you do it, Swede. If she is lying, I don't think I'd like to be the first one to know. Do you mind?"

"Of course not. What will you do in the meantime?"

Birch sighed. "There are other suspects to question. She's not the only one."

"But she is the only one with any connection at all to the Shirleys."

"Tomorrow," Birch said, ignoring Swede's comment, "I'll start interviewing the stagecoach drivers. I sure hope you don't find a connection, Swede."

That was the end of their conversation. The rest of the trip back to Grass Valley was filled with silence. Both men brooded over their own troubles.

The next morning, Swede began to investigate Lulu Montana's itinerary, wiring inquiries to all of the surrounding towns, starting with Nevada City. Once he had the dates of the towns in which she appeared, he put them together with the banks that had been robbed.

By late afternoon, a pattern had begun to emerge. Swede looked down at the two papers, side by side, filled with information. He blinked and rubbed the bridge of his nose, a headache throbbing in the back of his skull. It was no surprise, of course, but it was difficult for Swede to know how to handle it. How was he going to get Birch to believe that the woman he loved was lying to him? That would be the biggest task of the day.

CHAPTER 15

LULU sat on the edge of her bed in her barren little Emigrant Gap hotel room, brushing her hair. She wished there was a mirror. The problem with these fledgling boomtowns was they sometimes were so new that a good hotel hadn't been built yet. Lulu wasn't even sure there was a hotel in the mining camp she was going to, a place called Angels Camp. She usually avoided towns that small, but it was close by and she had to be there tomorrow night.

Of course, she couldn't complain. The smaller mining camps were sometimes the best places to sing. Not only was the audience starved for entertainment, but they showed their appreciation by showering her with gold nuggets. She could make a lot of money from drunken miners.

Maybe someday she'd have enough money to go to San Francisco, enough to stay in the finest hotel and dine in high-class restaurants, enough to meet and marry a wealthy man. Then she wouldn't have to travel from one stinking little mining camp to another.

Lulu sighed and thought of Jefferson Birch. Against her good judgment, she was becoming fond of him.

Lulu brushed her hair so fiercely that static built up, making her scalp tingle and her dark hair crackle with every stroke. She regretted the lies that she'd had to tell him.

His friend, Swede, had been more difficult to convince. He wasn't captivated by her. She didn't like him for that reason. She had no use for men who were not beguiled by her charms. But Lulu couldn't worry about Swede at the moment, although he was not a man who would easily give up, no matter what Birch said. She hoped Birch could handle him for her. After all, Birch was in charge of the investigation of the bank robberies. Swede was just assisting him.

Lulu put her brush on the bed beside her and began to smooth the worry lines that were slowly building up on her brow. She tried not to be too concerned about any problems that arose because she suspected that worry caused wrinkles. Her mother had aged fast, even though she died before she was thirty-five. She had spent most of her life worrying where the next meal would come from, worrying about raising her children, worrying about her husband's heavy drinking, worrying about fierce rains washing away their harvest. All that worrying had sent Lulu's mother, looking like an old woman before her time, to an early grave.

Lulu touched her fingertips to her brow and tried to massage the creases away. She knew that Swede, and eventually Birch, would find out the truth. And they would capture the Shirleys. However, by then, she would be miles away. In San Francisco.

Her brow furrowed again as she thought about the robberies. Lulu had one little concern: she hadn't been in Nevada City before that robbery took place. Could the Shirleys have held up that bank without her? Maybe they had gotten some information from another source and had gone ahead and robbed it. But it wasn't like them to kill someone. It had to be the work of another gang.

Lulu let her hands fall into her lap. She cocked her head slightly, trying to work it out in her head. If the Shirleys had robbed the Nevada City Bank, maybe they didn't need her anymore. Maybe they were making plans to work without her from now on.

Vardis, the oldest brother, had always liked her. She couldn't imagine Vardis cheating her out of her money.

And Clyde didn't have the brains God gave a chicken. He was just a big, dumb, good-natured fellow. But he had a soft spot for her as well because she had been married to his favorite brother, Emmet. Homer was a nervous one, and probably the most intelligent of the four brothers, which wasn't saying much. But he didn't have much presence, and no one took him seriously. Fergis was closest to Vardis. He was a crafty devil and he'd never liked Lulu much. When the brothers had decided to use Lulu, he had loudly objected to bringing her into the gang, even though her job was to find out when the best time was to rob a bank. Vardis might be influenced by him without Lulu there to defend herself. If anyone was trying to cut her out of the bank money, it would be Fergis.

Lulu sighed and picked up her hairbrush again. It would be no use in her worrying. She would find out the answer to some of her questions tomorrow night.

CHAPTER 16

BIRCH stared down at the paper Swede had just handed to him. It was undeniable proof of Lulu's treachery. Swede had practically dragged him into the sheriff's office an hour ago and placed the information in front of him.

"There had better be a good reason for this," Birch had grumbled as he dismounted Cactus and followed Swede inside.

Now it was here before him. As he stared at the paper, Swede, who had been silently sitting in a nearby chair, finally spoke up. "Well, what do you think?"

"It doesn't prove anything," Birch grumbled. "She was in most of the towns right before a bank was robbed, but she wasn't in Nevada City. In fact, she was seventy-five miles away in Oroville."

"I know," Swede replied, getting up and pacing. "That didn't make any sense to me, either, unless the Shirley gang didn't rob that bank. Your eyewitness could have been mistaken. It wouldn't be the first time."

Birch was about to admit that he'd had some doubts about the Shirley gang robbing the Nevada City Bank, but Harold Valentine suddenly opened the door and strode inside. "I see you're hard at work, Mr. Birch."

Birch stood up and introduced Swede to the owner of the Grass Valley Bank.

"Have you any new information on the Shirleys? Rhodes and I are getting anxious," Valentine said, clasping his hands behind his back. "It's been about a week since you began your investigation and we haven't seen any results."

Swede turned to watch Birch's response. Birch looked

down at the information on the desk beneath his hand and hardened himself. "We—" He hesitated, closed his eyes for a moment, then went on. "We have a lead. Her name is Lulu Montana and she travels around, singing in saloons. I think she meets stagecoach drivers or telegraph operators in these saloons, and when they have a few drinks, they tell her when a payroll is coming into a bank. Then she passes it on to the Shirleys. Swede and I are going up to Emigrant Gap to question her."

Clearly delighted with the results, Valentine clapped his hands together. "Well, you've made more progress than either Rhodes or myself could have hoped for. What about the men who gave her the information? Can you find out their names?"

Birch and Swede looked at each other. Swede spoke up. "That may be more difficult. Even if she's willing to cooperate, Lulu Montana might not be able to remember their names or what they looked like. The men could be associated with the different banks or they could be the stagecoach drivers."

Birch added, "Or it could be they are the men who pick up the payrolls. They might have come in a day early and gotten drunk at the saloon where she worked." He shook his head. "No, Mr. Valentine. You're asking the impossible. We can get a confession out of Lulu Montana, we can capture the Shirleys for you, but I don't think it would be worth my time or yours for Swede and me to find out who was indiscreet. You would have them fired, and someone else just as careless would take their place."

"I'm not talking about finding out every man who has been talking. Just the men who gave information to this Lulu Montana in the Grass Valley and Nevada City bank robberies. After all, we're the ones paying for your services. If the other banks want to hire you to find out—"

Birch glanced at Swede for his reaction. Swede

shrugged. "We can try," Birch finally conceded. "But our priority is to find the Shirleys and bring them back here."

"Fair enough," Harold Valentine conceded. After a few more pleasantries, the bank owner left.

"I guess we'd better saddle up your horse," Birch said to Swede, "and ride up to Emigrant Gap."

"That took a lot of courage, Birch," Swede replied. "I know she meant something to you."

Birch didn't reply immediately. He adjusted his hat and started for the door, then hesitated and said, "She still does."

CHAPTER 17

BY the time Birch and Swede arrived in Emigrant Gap, the flickering yellow flames from kerosene lanterns dotted the main street. The night air had become chilly enough for Birch to turn his collar up. Howls of laughter came from the saloon down the street. Screams of laughter pierced the darkness. As they passed a whorehouse, a miner staggered or was pushed out of the door. A giggling woman followed, waving what looked like a limp red rag and calling out, "Sam! Don't forget your longjohns."

The miner turned around and managed to reply, "Yeah, thanks, Gertie," and snatched them from her hand.

Exchanging amused looks, Birch and Swede went on, finally coming to the saloon. The place was packed with men and the pungent smell of rye, whiskey, and beer. Unable to find a table, Swede and Birch went up to the bar to order their drinks. Birch looked around, but didn't spot Lulu.

As Swede ordered two whiskeys from the bartender, he asked, "Is Lulu Montana singing tonight?"

The bartender sloppily poured the liquor while he shook his head. "She's gone."

"Gone? Gone where?" Birch asked sharply.

The bartender gave him a funny look and replied, "Take it easy, stranger. When you're finished with your whiskey, just ride over to Angels Camp, about ten miles from here. She's singing for the miners over there."

The two men drank the fiery whiskey in one gulp, then left. It was a bright moonlit night, easy to see the road in

111

the dark, and they reached Angels Camp in fifteen minutes.

Angels Camp was much smaller than Emigrant Gap. There were no permanent buildings; mostly tents were set up around a campfire. There was a larger tent beyond the dimly lit camp. Miners were gathered under the open-sided tent, bottles of whiskey in hand. The inside of the tent was bright from kerosene lanterns. A few tables were scattered near the front of the tent where Lulu was singing, but most of the customers were standing. There was no real bar and no glasses to be found. Instead, customers bought bottles of rotgut whiskey from a man who stood near a supply wagon.

Lulu was standing on a shaky-looking wooden platform with a fiddler on either side of her for accompaniment. Birch and Swede listened to the music, sharing a bottle between them. Just as she ended a song, Birch felt Swede's elbow in his ribs.

"Look over there," Swede said, pointing toward the tent entrance. Four scruffy men were standing just inside the tent. One man had a dark beard and wore a fringed buckskin coat; another wore a large shapeless hat with leather thongs wound around it, feathers and beads dangling over the brim.

The one in the big hat headed toward the stage, the others following his lead. One of the men walked with a limp.

"That has to be the Shirley brothers," Swede muttered.

Birch watched them approach Lulu, his heart sinking as she greeted them with a smile and motioned them to a table that had just become empty. Birch and Swede quickly turned away when she looked in their direction. Birch and Swede were standing in the dark end of the tent, so the chances of Lulu spotting them in such a crowd were pretty slim.

"What do you want to do?" Swede asked.

Birch leaned against a nearby tent pole, watching the four brothers and Lulu. "Just keep watch. When the Shirleys leave, we'll follow them."

Privately, Birch had hoped that he wouldn't have to confront Lulu. Yes, she had lied to him, but Birch was ready to believe that there was a good reason for that. Maybe the Shirleys had some hold over her. Maybe she was afraid of them and had been forced into working for them. But as he watched her with the Shirleys, he saw no indication that she was anything other than comfortable with her in-laws, the same men she swore she had not seen for many years.

The discussion got heated. The man in the buckskin jacket, Birch figured he had to be Vardis, banged his fist on the table, leaning over Lulu to make his point. When Vardis was finished, he sat down, a smug look on his face. Lulu stood up, her mouth set in a thin line—apparently their talk was over.

The four men got up. Vardis reached over to pat Lulu's shoulder. She remained motionless, not looking at them. Birch waited for the Shirleys to leave before he and Swede followed. In the darkness outside the tent, Birch paused to look back at Lulu. She was staring out over the crowd, her eyes appearing to rest on him, but he knew she could not see him. Even if she did, he could see that her mind was not on the here and now. She was brooding about something else altogether.

Birch and Swede rode after the Shirleys. The moon had risen higher, giving out an intensely bright light to navigate by. The hills were deceitful when seen from far away. They appeared to be gentle undulations that were low enough to climb if a traveler needed to see where he was going. But as they approached the hills, they realized that if they lost the gang, there wouldn't be time to climb to the top of a hill. It would take at least ten or fifteen minutes, and by then, the gang would be too far away. Besides, they might be spotted by the Shirleys in the intense white moonlight.

Instead, Birch and Swede relied on instinct and the faint trail that led them farther from civilization. Eventually they came to a spot where the trail split.

The two men stopped, Birch dismounting and peering closely at the tracks. "Both sets are fresh," he announced. "They must have split up. Maybe one of them caught sight of us following them and they decided to throw us off the track."

He stood up and squinted into the distance. Swede stayed on his horse.

"Well, what do you think we should do now?" he asked Birch.

"I'll take this trail and you take the other. If you come across their hideout, don't try anything by yourself. We'll meet up back here in an hour."

Swede dismounted and started following the tracks that went off to the west. Birch watched his friend go before turning to the other tracks. The hour went by fast. The trail Birch followed doubled back, and he found himself back where he'd started.

"Damn," he muttered under his breath. He looked in the direction that Swede had gone and wondered if he should pursue him. Maybe he could catch up to Swede and save some time in catching the outlaws. He began tracking. Soon the trail became a muddle, going off in different directions. Birch was unable to continue, so he turned back, certain that Swede would be at the designated spot waiting for him. He hoped his partner had had better luck.

The moonlight still shone crystal clear on the land. Swede was not there waiting for Birch. After waiting for fifteen more minutes, Birch began to wonder what might have happened. Swede could have gotten lost, but he didn't think that was likely. The big Norwegian might have captured the four Shirleys single-handed and could be heading back to Grass Valley at this very moment, but again, Birch thought that wasn't very probable. Swede knew that he was to meet Birch here. Even if he'd caught the Shirleys, he wouldn't start back to Grass Valley without a second guard. No, the most likely answer was that the Shirleys who had doubled back on Birch had come across Swede. He had probably been caught by them.

Birch considered his options. He could continue to look for a trail, but he'd already done that and had been thwarted by the Shirleys, who doubled back and confused the trail. He only had one slim hope, and she was in Angels Camp. He wheeled Cactus around, pointing toward the miner's camp and spurred his horse into a gallop. Birch could only hope that Lulu would help him.

CHAPTER 18

SWEDE felt someone shove the cold metal barrel of a gun against the back of his head. "Hold it right there, mister," said a thin, flat, nasal voice. "Don't make me do anything you'll regret." He stepped into Swede's vision, the man with the fringed buckskin jacket. Vardis Shirley, Swede thought. With a cautious eye on Swede, Vardis ordered, "Now toss your gun away from you."

Swede complied. He wasn't sure how it had been done, but somehow, the Shirleys had figured out that they were being followed. Something rustled in nearby bushes. Vardis whipped his head around. "What was that?" he asked sharply. He nervously trained his gun at the center of Swede's chest.

"Just some night animal," Swede replied in a calm, deliberate tone. "Probably hunting for food."

"Don't play dumb with me," Vardis said with a sneer. "I know there was two of you. Where's the other one?"

"We split up. He's probably heading back to Grass Valley right now. Maybe he's going to get the law."

Vardis poked his captive in the ribs with his gun and said, "Come on, git goin'. I'm takin' you back to the others. We'll all decide what to do with you then."

They started forward. Swede had been waiting for an opportunity to jump Vardis, and now seemed as good a time as any. As he turned in the direction Vardis had indicated, Swede pretended to stumble. Then he shoved his shoulder into the outlaw's side, throwing him off balance. Swede staggered as well, but he managed to grab Vardis's gun hand. The outlaw dropped his gun. Vardis

116

hit out with his free fist, catching Swede in the face, then aimed a kick at his shins. Swede sidestepped the attack and lunged for Vardis, grabbing him by the neck. The two men fell to the ground in their skirmish, Vardis grappling for his fallen gun and Swede shaking the life out of the outlaw. Finally, Vardis had no more struggle in him and became as limp as a dead snake. Swede rolled him over on his stomach and started to pull out the handcuffs when he heard another voice say, "Git up offa my brother or you'll be seeing moonlight out of your belly."

Swede did as he was instructed. When he turned around, he was face-to-face with another brother, the one with the limp. He was skinny with a prominent Adam's apple that kept bobbing up and down. Perspiration had plastered his shaggy hair to his forehead.

Gasping, sputtering, and coughing came from the prone man behind Swede.

"You all right, Vardis?" the boy asked, not taking his eyes off Swede.

"Right as rain now that you come along, Homer," Vardis said in a strangled tone. "You shore took your time about it." Swede could hear Vardis's knees crack as he got up off the ground. "Where were you?"

"I kinda got lost, Vardis. You was goin' too fast for me."

Vardis came into view and clapped his younger brother on the back. "Well, no matter now. You done found your way. If you'd been any longer, I mighta been on my way to Grass Valley with this here lawman."

"What we gonna do with him, Vardis?" Homer asked eagerly.

Vardis, noticing Swede watching the boy, snatched the gun from Homer's hands. "You go tie him up."

Homer's face lit up. "Sure, Vardis." He went over to Swede but was apparently at a loss as to what to use. Then his eyes fell on the handcuffs that Swede had been about to use on Vardis. They had fallen to the ground in the struggle and he snatched them up. "We can use these on him, can't we, Vardis?"

"Go ahead, boy." Vardis grinned nastily.

Swede felt his wrists tethered by his own manacles behind his back.

"Now what, Vardis?"

"We take this prisoner back to our shack." With the barrel of his gun, Vardis prodded Swede to get moving.

The trail was faint, almost nonexistent, and they had to ford two small creeks. By this time, Swede had given up any hope of Birch finding him. He would have to get himself out of this one alone. Thoughts of his wife, Greta, and their unborn baby flashed through Swede's mind.

The hideout was exactly what Vardis had described—a rickety, tumbledown miner's shack. Some of the slats had rotted away, leaving the cabin walls open enough to see the light of a kerosene lamp shining from within. Swede slowed down, but was again nudged by Vardis's gun to step up to the door. Homer hurried ahead and opened the door.

The sound of shotguns being primed to shoot greeted Swede as he loomed in the doorway. Fortunately, Vardis called out, "Don't shoot. It's just us, boys. We brought us a prisoner."

The two men in the cabin walked across the packed dirt floor toward the entrance. In the bright moonlight that slipped between the open spaces of the shack's walls, he saw the pale countenances of the other two brothers, Fergis and Clyde. One brother was short and chubby with a baby face. He was attempting to grow a mustache, but all he could manage was a few wispy sprouts above his soft lip. The other brother was lean and leathery with mean eyes and a chin that was dotted with stubble.

It was hard for Swede to believe these men were brothers until he looked at the small, wide-spaced eyes and the long, thin nose that they all had in common. He still wasn't sure which of the two unidentified bothers was which yet, but he was certain that he'd find out before the night was over — if he lived that long.

The lean brother scratched his whiskery jaw and walked around Swede, examining him. "What're we supposed to do with him, Vardis? Where'd you find him?"

"He was out there prowling around. He must have recognized us back at Angels Camp. I guess he got onto our trail before we got a chance to confuse the tracks." Vardis rubbed his neck, looking ruefully at Swede, and said, "If it warn't for the quick thinking of your brother, Homer, I bet I'd be on my way back to Grass Valley to face trial for those bank robberies."

Swede couldn't help adding, "And the murder of a bank clerk."

The four brothers stared at him as if he were crazy. Clyde, or Fergis, turned to Vardis and asked, "What's he talkin' about?"

Vardis shrugged wearily. "Don't know, boys. But I'm tired. Let's talk about this in the morning. Shackle him to that chair over there."

Swede was led over to the middle of the room and his manacled wrists uncomfortably tied to a chair with rope.

"We'll all take shifts guarding him while the rest of us get some sleep," Vardis ordered. "Fergis, you take the first watch."

The lean brother with the whiskers stepped forward and grabbed a chair, turning it around and sitting in it with his elbows resting across the back of the chair, his arms cradling his shotgun. His mouth was set in a straight line and his eyes glinted meanly. The other three men took up blankets from a corner. The two younger ones headed for a pile of straw in one corner of the room and Vardis laid down in the shack's only bed.

Except for the occasional sound of a chirping cricket and the hoot of a night owl, Swede heard only loud breathing from the bed and the pile of straw. He thought about getting Fergis to talk, but the few times Clyde and Homer murmured to each other, Vardis sat up in his bed and snapped, "Stop it, you two, and get some sleep. You're goin' to need it for your watch." Soon, the cabin was filled with snoring and snorting from all three brothers. Swede settled down for the long night ahead.

CHAPTER 19

BIRCH was back in Angels Camp less than fifteen minutes later. He found Lulu still under the tent, entertaining miners. When she caught sight of his grim face, she quickly finished up her song, gathered up the gold that had been tossed at her, and headed toward him. He could see a reluctance in her movements, but his urgency must have made her curious.

She looked delighted to see him. "So you couldn't keep away from me. It's good to see you again, Birch."

Unsmiling, he replied, "Swede and I were here earlier tonight, but you were busy."

Her smile became uncertain, her eyes unreadable. "Well," Lulu said cautiously, "I am working. But you could have waited until I took a break."

"You already had company," he replied evenly.

She looked away, her first sign of nervousness. "I don't know what you're talking about."

"I'm talking about the Shirleys. They came here to see you."

Lulu looked around, then took him by the arm and led him away from the tent. Her eyes glittered. Two hard lines appeared on either side of her mouth. Her voice was harsh. "Okay, so they were here. What was I supposed to do, arrest them?"

"Did they tell you to keep an eye on me?" Birch asked. "Or was that your own idea. That's why you allowed me to court you."

Lulu crossed her arms and turned away from Birch. When she spoke, her voice was cold. "That first night, I saw you talking to that little man. After you left, I bought him a drink and he told me about you. I guessed that you would eventually find out about my past, so I encouraged you to visit me." She paused, then her voice was softer as she added, "You may not believe this, but in spite of everything, I grew fond of you."

"They have Swede."

She looked at him with a startled expression, which was quickly replaced by obstinacy. "You must have followed them when they left here." Lulu stamped her foot and crossed her arms. "Why did you have to ruin everything?"

Birch grabbed her by the shoulders and shook her. "I need to know where to find them."

Lulu shook her head slowly. "I can't tell you."

"Can't—or won't?"

Tearing herself away from Birch's grip, Lulu narrowed her eyes and replied, "What difference does it make? Your friend is gone. He'll be all right if you just leave. Why don't you go back to Grass Valley? Better yet, why don't you go back to wherever it was you came from in the first place? Just leave me alone."

"I can't do that, Lulu," Birch said, taking a pair of handcuffs from his pocket.

She stepped back warily. "What are you doing?"

He clipped one cuff around her right wrist. "I'm arresting you for abetting a number of bank robberies—"

"I'll scream," she warned.

"Go ahead. I'll explain that I'm a deputy sheriff." He flashed his badge at her.

Lulu lowered her eyes and her voice. "Don't do this to me, Birch."

"Lulu, Swede is in danger. I need to find him. I know you and Swede don't like each other, but he's my friend. If you won't help me, I'll take you down to the jail. Maybe the Shirleys will come to your rescue."

There was a moment's hesitation, then she heaved a

defeated sigh. "All right. You win. I'll take you there. But you have to promise me that you'll let me go if you do catch the Shirleys. My part in the bank robberies was small compared to theirs."

"I can't make any promises," he said. "You'd better pray Swede is alive when we get there."

"Oh, I wouldn't worry about that." Holding up her right wrist, Lulu added, "Now get these things off me or we're not going anywhere."

Reluctantly Birch obliged, then swung Lulu up on Cactus, positioned himself behind her, and spurred his horse in the direction of the hills. The moon hung low in the night sky but still lit the path that took them back to where Birch and Swede had split up.

Lulu looked around, then pointed straight ahead. "This way."

The trail took Birch through familiar territory until they reached the area where part of the gang doubled back and confused the tracks. "This is as far as I got," Birch said.

Lulu nodded silently and indicated the path to be taken. When they reached a stream, Lulu said, "We have to go across here." Cactus waded across the shallow water, the creek never coming any higher than his shanks. On the other side, there was a steep bank to climb.

Lulu directed Birch to follow the stream to the left for a quarter of a mile, then away from the creek until they came to a second brook, which was half the size of the first one. Again, Cactus forded this one with little trouble, and they climbed a small hill. When they reached the top, Lulu gestured to the other side.

"The boys have a shack down there." She swung down from Cactus and turned to Birch, her hands on her hips. "Now what are you going to do?"

Birch hesitated. He'd been thinking about what to do from the moment they left Angels Camp. His first purpose was to free Swede, if he was still alive. From there, they could take the Shirleys together. But he hadn't come to a decision about Lulu Montana. He couldn't risk the chance that she would warn her in-laws. How far could he trust her?

She was still staring at him with an ironic smile twisting her lovely features when he pulled out the handcuffs. Her expression hardened as it dawned on her that Birch meant to cuff her to a tree. She shook her head and started backing up. "No. You're not using those things on me again."

Birch lunged for her, but she slipped away and ran down the hill. He paused, finally deciding that going after her would take away precious time from his original purpose: setting Swede free. Besides, she had run in the opposite direction of the cabin, so chances were that Lulu planned to get as far away as possible. He slipped the handcuffs back into his saddlebag. He wouldn't need them just yet.

Next, he led Cactus halfway down the hill and tethered the horse to the lowest branch of a tree, keeping his horse out of sight of the shack. Finally, Birch crept toward the cabin, his gun at the ready.

CHAPTER 20

SWEDE had begun to nod off when the first gunshot cracked through the air above the cabin. His instinct for self-preservation drove Swede to fall on his side, chair and all. A shooting pain went through his shoulder as he made impact with the hardened earth, but with bullets flying around, he now had a better chance of staying alive than if he were still sitting upright.

The sharp sound of gunfire woke the Shirleys up fast. Clyde, who had taken the second shift and promptly nodded off, was now wide awake, swinging his shotgun at random corners of the cabin, as if he was ready to shoot at anything that moved. Vardis had slipped out of bed into a crouch, his gun cocked and ready. Fergis and Homer grabbed their nearby weapons and crawled across the floor toward their older brother.

"What's going on, Vardis?" Homer croaked in a sleep-hoarse voice.

"How the hell should I know? Maybe some dang fool's out there night hunting." His eyes shifted to Swede's prone figure. "Maybe it's the other fella that was with our friend here," he suggested slyly.

Another couple of shots sounded. They were so close together that it was hard to tell if one or two people were shooting.

"Sounds like more than one gun out there, Vardis," Clyde piped up nervously.

Vardis's eyes narrowed, gleaming craftily, as he thought this one over. "Don't think so. I'd be willing to bet it's only one man. Clyde," he said sharply, "you stay here and guard our man in the chair. The rest of you will come with me. When we get outside, we'll spread out." The others nodded and crept to the door with their older brother. Swede twisted his confined body slowly around to face the door. Clyde remained hunched over, a terrified expression on his face, watching his prisoner.

Swede heard four gunshots; the smell of gunsmoke curling in through the cracks in the walls of the miner's shack told him that the Shirleys were firing blindly into the hills to draw out the shooter. Swede smiled to himself as he imagined the nervous outlaws swinging their guns around and firing at each other. He sobered up after imagining one of them gunning down Swede's only hope: Jefferson Birch. He soon dismissed this notion; Birch was much too smart for these mountain folk.

Swede was so caught up in his thoughts that he almost didn't notice the movement. The door slowly inched open little by little. Clyde must have sensed that something was amiss because he started to turn his head toward the entrance.

"What do you and the others plan to do with me?" Swede asked.

Clyde turned his vacant face toward Swede, proving that he was easily distracted and not too bright. "Do with you?" he repeated blankly.

"You can't keep me tied up here forever. You'll either have to kill me to silence me, or let me go somewhere in the middle of nowhere. Either way, you'll still be wanted by the law."

Clyde frowned. "That's the second time you've mentioned killin'—" He didn't get to finish his sentence. Birch was now behind him, his gun aimed at Clyde's fat neck. The young Shirley's eyes widened as he comprehended what was happening, and he slowly lowered his shotgun to the floor.

"That's right," Birch said in a low voice. "Now let's get my friend out of that chair."

"Vardis has the key," Clyde said meekly. In the dim light of the cabin, Swede thought he detected a faint sheen of perspiration on the young man's upper lip.

Swede nodded to Birch. "He's right. We'll have to shoot through the links of these handcuffs."

Before Swede could warn Birch, the door opened wide, revealing the other three Shirleys, all brandishing their shotguns and looking very unhappy. Lulu trailed behind them. Vardis silently appraised Birch, then said to his brothers, "Looks like we got us another one." He turned back to Birch and said, "There's three of us and one of you. So I'd advise that you drop your gun, stranger."

Birch paused, then nodded his defeat without a word. He looked at Lulu as he dropped his gun, but her eyes were downcast.

The Shirleys and Lulu entered the cabin. A very shaken Clyde collected his shotgun and Birch's Colt. "You made it back just in time, Vardis."

Fergis walked up to Clyde and backhanded his brother. Clyde put a hand to his reddened cheek, his fat lower lip quivering. "Why'd you do that, Ferg? What'd I do?"

"You let this man sneak up on you, that's what you done," Fergis hissed.

"Leave him alone, Fergis," Vardis ordered sharply. "It all worked out all right."

Fergis turned on his older brother and snapped, "But what about the next time? You've always been too easy on him, Vardis. Daddy wouldn't of been that way."

Vardis nodded to Clyde and said, "You learned your lesson, didn't you, boy?"

Clyde nodded silently. Vardis nodded, apparently satisfied. He gestured to Birch. "Tie him up. If he don't have any manacles on him, there's some rope over in the corner."

Like a dog trying to please his master, Clyde inspected Birch for handcuffs, and when he found none, he trotted over to the corner and brought back a length of hemp. Fergis snatched the rope away from him and tied Birch's hands behind his back, yanking so viciously on the knots that Swede thought he saw Birch wince. Swede turned to look at Lulu, who sat on the edge of the bed, her expression unreadable. She shifted uncomfortably under his gaze and avoided looking at either Birch or Swede.

Suddenly, she stood up, anger sweeping her features. "What did you expect, Birch?" she asked in a loud, exasperated tone. "You thought that if I fell in love with you, I'd gladly hand over my in-laws to you?" Her hands were balled into tight fists and she turned her back to everyone. In the murky light, it was hard to tell, but Swede could have sworn Lulu's shoulders were shaking, as if she were quietly crying.

CHAPTER 21

MORNING dawned gray and dreary. Lulu had already risen and was making a bland breakfast of sourdough biscuits and beans. The Shirleys had agreed that the woman should take the bed, and she had slept as well as could be expected under the circumstances.

As she glanced over at the hunched over prisoners she became indignant all over again. How dare Jefferson Birch put her in this position. Now she was forced to watch him and his friend trussed up, and she had no idea if they'd live or die. She didn't trust the Shirleys like she used to. Jefferson Birch had put doubts in her mind.

The trouble had started when she heard about the bank robbery in Nevada City. Before then, Lulu had gotten along fine with the Shirleys. Although she didn't care much for Fergis, Clyde and Homer were sweet and Vardis had always treated her like a sister. Lulu had never had any illusions about the Shirley family, even when she married Emmet. They made their living by lying, cheating, and stealing, but they had never killed. Daddy Shirley would have no truck with a murderer. "The Bible says killin's a sin," Daddy Shirley would always say. When Lulu would point out that lying, cheating, and stealing were not virtues, he always replied, "Maybe, but killin's a hangin' offense."

And that was the Shirleys' code—until now. Since lying was one of the things a Shirley came by naturally, Lulu could never be sure if Vardis was telling the truth when he told her that they hadn't robbed the Nevada City Bank.

129

And now with Daddy Shirley and Emmet dead, maybe killing was no longer out of bounds for the Shirleys.

Lulu had met a famous gunman once a few years ago. His eyes had been dead like two cold agates. Fergis had eyes like that and a quick temper to go with it. Lulu could imagine him shooting someone down. She stirred the beans to keep them from burning on the bottom of the cast iron pot.

From over in the corner where the brothers huddled in the straw and blankets, Vardis ordered Clyde to get a couple of buckets of water from the creek nearby. The pudgy young man struggled up, pulled his pants on over his longjohns and, scratching his belly, shuffled across to the door. She heard the sound of metal pails clinking together outside as Clyde did his chore.

Her thoughts turned to this youngest of the brothers. Maybe Clyde had shot the teller in Nevada City. He was young and less experienced at robbery. She'd heard Fergis complain that Clyde got nervous when they held up a bank and someday he might get someone killed. In either case, she could well imagine the rest of the brothers covering up for the one who shot and killed an innocent bystander, whether on purpose or by accident. As for Vardis and Homer, she couldn't see either of them deviating from the code they had come to live by. Vardis was too set in his ways, and Homer idolized his older brother, trying very hard to live up to the code.

Birch stirred, and Lulu started to go over to him, but movement from across the room told her that the other Shirleys were starting to stir. She began to think that she'd made a mistake by turning on Birch. Maybe she should have let him free Swede and left the brothers to take their chances with the law. She could have been far away from here by now if she hadn't panicked and run to Vardis last night.

Fergis strolled over. "Smells good." He poured himself a

mug of coffee, eyeing Lulu as if he could read her thoughts. She moved restlessly under his gaze, spooning beans and biscuits onto a plate and handing it to him without a word. The rest of the men came over and helped themselves.

When everyone had eaten their fill and pushed back from the table, Lulu turned to Vardis and said, "What about them?" She pointed to Birch and Swede, both bleary-eyed from an uncomfortable night in straight-backed chairs. "They have to eat as well. Who's going to feed them?"

Vardis rubbed his beard in thought, then, with a gleam in his eye, replied, "You do it. You'll feed 'em. I got to go see about the horses." With that, he rose from his chair and walked out the door, Fergis following him.

Her heart sank. She didn't know if she could face Birch's impassive face, but she steeled herself and loaded up a couple of plates and poured coffee into two mugs.

Together, Clyde and Homer picked up the two captives, chairs and all, and set them at the table in front of the full plates Lulu had placed there moments before. She sat reluctantly between the prisoners and began to feed them as quietly as possible. Fergis got back before Vardis and sat in a chair, a stalk of grass between his teeth. He continued unabashedly to stare in her direction, an amused smirk twisting his features. Occasionally, she turned and stared hard at him, hoping he'd get the hint and go find something else to do. Instead, her attentions seemed to keep him riveted to his seat, enjoying the show that she and the two captives put on.

"Coffee's too hot," Birch murmured, turning his face away from the scalding steam as she lifted the mug to his lips.

"Sorry," she whispered, setting the mug back down to cool.

"I don't suppose you'll loosen these bonds for me," Birch muttered bitterly.

"You forced me into helping you and got yourself into this mess," she answered in a low fierce tone, "so don't try to make me feel guilty."

Lulu turned abruptly and fed the quiet Swede for a few minutes in an effort to ignore Birch's presence. His silence made the closeness all the more apparent to her, and with this realization, she became furious. Suddenly, she was angry with Vardis for ordering her to spoon-feed these two men and angry with Fergis for standing by and watching her attempts. And she was annoyed by Clyde and Homer, who pretended to ignore the scene in the shack, but who couldn't help sneaking furtive glances in their direction.

Vardis came back inside, smelling of hay and horse manure. "It's a brisk morning," he announced to no one in particular. Lulu stood up and cleared the table, taking the plates and mugs outside to wash in a bucket of water that Clyde had gotten from the stream before breakfast.

When she got back inside, the brothers were sitting around the table, Birch and Swede back in the middle of the shack. All eyes turned toward her.

Her mouth tightened a little. "What's this, a meeting?" Lulu asked drily.

Looking more serious than usual, Vardis cleared his throat and said, "I think you'd better come sit down, Louise." Lulu gritted her teeth. She hated her Christian name. "We got to talk a few things out," he went on to explain, "like what we're gonna do with these here fellas."

CHAPTER 22

WHEN Swede had woken up that morning, he had noticed that his shoulder was throbbing. His neck was stiff from falling asleep in the chair, and when he had begun to reach up and massage the muscles, he realized that his wrists were handcuffed to a chair. Swede had never thought the simple act of wielding an axe would appeal to him in the way it did right then. His arms ached to swing it high over his head, cleanly splitting cords of wood. He wanted to be back in Grant's Pass with his wife and unborn child. What would happen to them if he didn't come back? He tried not to think about the possibilities.

Breakfast had been filled with tension. Lulu had mechanically shoveled beans into his mouth and held biscuits up for him to eat. He especially hated to drink hot coffee as if he were an infant. All the while, he had been aware that she was disconcerted to be sitting next to Jefferson Birch, the man she had betrayed. Maybe it was wishful thinking, but Swede thought she was starting to regret that betrayal. Tiny furrows in her brow appeared whenever she looked over at the Shirley brothers.

Now they were having a family meeting around the table. Lulu had just come in from washing the plates and mugs, and reluctantly sat with the outlaws, studiously ignoring both Birch and Swede. Vardis stood at the head of the table, his voice carrying stridently beyond the circle of brothers and Lulu. "We got to decide what to do with these here fellas. But first, we got to get a few things out of the way after our talk last night." He looked straight at Lulu. She paled, obviously shaken from the meeting in

Angels Camp last night. "Lulu, you practically accused us of dealing you out of the robberies with that Nevada City job. I think I can say, for all of us, that we was hurt that you would think we was capable of doing such a thing."

Swede watched her struggle with an expression that was somewhere between terrified and chastised. "Vardis," she replied in a small voice, "I just asked if you robbed that bank without my help."

Fergis stood up, looking fierce, and said, "You know that we don't hold with killin'. A man was killed in that robbery, and you know damn well we won't have nothin' to do with a hangin' offense."

She inclined her head meekly. "I should have realized that, Fergis. But I guess I thought, well, with Emmet and Daddy Shirley gone, and us out here in California, things might have changed."

"Our code hasn't changed," Fergis replied curtly. There was a short silence, then he looked at her slyly and added, "'Course, there's nothin' that says that you couldn't of met up with another gang of outlaws and told 'em about Nevada City."

"I wasn't anywhere near Nevada City, Fergis Shirley," Lulu snapped. She turned toward Birch and Swede. "Isn't that right, Birch?"

"That's right," he acknowledged tiredly. "Swede and I inquired into where Lulu had been during the robbery. She was in Oroville, seventy-five miles away. She couldn't have traveled to Nevada City to rob a bank, then gotten back in time to sing that night."

Swede shifted in his chair, longing to break his manacles and stretch his arms. The arguments went on for a few more minutes, both Lulu and Vardis finally settling into a wary alliance.

"Now we got to figure out what to do with these two," Vardis said, nodding in Swede and Birch's direction. "Any suggestions?"

Fergis spoke up. "Seems to me that we got to leave this area. We've been to every bank worth robbing around here anyway. So we have only two choices. Either leave 'em here or take 'em with us."

Vardis scratched at his beard thoughtfully. "I think you're right, Fergis. Sounds about like the only choices we got. Let's see, we got four horses between us, and the horse that the big blond fella came riding in on." He looked over at Birch, his eyes narrowing with thought. "That's enough horses for all of us. We better find the other fella's horse so's they can't follow us if they get free. I bet you we'll come up with a horse tied up somewheres nearby."

An overexcited Clyde piped up, "When I got the water this morning, I thought I heard a horse whinny up on the hill."

Vardis nodded. "Clyde, why don't you go lookin' for it, then. Homer can go with you. And give it some water and oats when you come across it. Don't need no dead horse-flesh around here when we can always use a fresh horse." He slapped his hand on the table surface. "Well, that's decided it then. We'll leave these fellas here. Don't have enough horses to go around with Lulu taking one."

Swede saw Lulu's eyes widen. "You want me to go with you?" she asked.

"Well, of course, sister," Vardis replied expansively. "You didn't think we'd leave you here by yourself, did you? What if these two prisoners get loose with you still here? Emmet would've never forgiven me if I didn't take care of his wife." He came over and put an arm around her shoulder. "We'll leave after our midday meal."

Lulu seemed to shrink back from his touch, her eyes inadvertently looking in Birch's direction. Swede thought she had the look of a cornered animal, but she managed to smile for Vardis.

For the rest of the morning, one or more brothers were

in the cabin, and Lulu kept herself busy. Finally, Lulu and Clyde were alone with the prisoners.

"Clyde," Lulu said.

He turned toward her, an eager-to-please puppy dog expression on his face.

"Clyde," she said again, this time softer. She moved closer. "I'm awful worried that I'll be left here in this cabin with those two. I mean, with all you men getting ready to travel, there may come a point when I need protection. What if one of them gets loose? Can you lend me one of your guns for protection?"

Clyde looked worried. "I don't know, Lulu. I think you better ask Vardis. He'd know if it was all right for you to carry a weapon." He shook his head slowly. "If it was up to me, I'd give you a gun. But I don't think Vardis thinks we can spare a gun."

"Did I hear my name?" Vardis was standing just inside the door.

Clyde turned around. "Oh, hi, Vardis. Lulu here just was asking if she could have a gun for protection. In case one of them fellas gets loose."

Vardis strode over to Lulu, who cowered under his scrutiny. "No, I don't think that would be a good idea." He looked over at Birch and Swede and added, "If they get loose, they'd just take the gun away from you. I think you'd be better off without a weapon." He grinned at her. "That's what we're here for, to protect you." Vardis took the blankets from the corner and started to leave again, pausing at the door to say, "You know, I'm getting mighty hungry. Maybe you better cook up some of that bacon."

Swede watched Lulu's shoulders slump as she started to pull out provisions for the noon meal. When she came to the bacon, she swore softly, then called out, "I need a knife, Clyde, to cut the bacon."

He looked over at her with a worried expression and replied, "You can't just fry it up whole, can you?"

Lulu gave him a stern look and mildly mocked him. "No, I can't just fry it up whole. It would take too long to cook, and it would get burned on the outside while the inside still had to cook." She went over to him and stuck out her hand. "Hand it over."

"I don't know if this is such a good idea," Clyde said meekly, but he was already fumbling for it.

"You know Vardis just told me to start cooking the meal," she told him firmly.

"Maybe I should cut the bacon," Clyde said stubbornly, holding it back.

Lulu took the knife from his hand and laughed lightly. "I bet you've never cut bacon in your life." She inspected the weapon and, with a little smile toward Clyde, said, "This knife still looks like new. I bet you hardly ever use it, Clyde."

Clyde turned red and, lowering his eyes, muttered, "It's new, Lulu. I just bought it last week."

Since last night, Swede had come to the conclusion that Clyde was the least experienced outlaw of the bunch, but now he realized that the youngest brother was also something of an incompetent. He turned his head and locked eyes with Birch, who gave him a little nod.

Lulu was slicing the bacon now. She looked over at the bucket. "Clyde, I think we need more water. Can you go down to the creek for me?"

Clyde looked dubious. "Someone has to stay here to guard them, Lulu. You know that. You just told me you were worried."

She looked up impatiently and replied, "Well, if someone doesn't go down to the creek and get some water, there'll be no coffee with your meal. If you're so worried about leaving them, just go on outside and call in Homer or Fergis to watch these two. I'll be all right for a few minutes."

Clyde picked up the bucket and walked outside without

another word. Swede saw Lulu wipe the knife off and tuck it into her pocket, her eyes on the door the whole time. Homer came in and nodded to her before sitting down.

When the meal was ready, she turned to Homer and said, "Go tell the others that dinner's ready."

"All right, Lulu," Homer said. As soon as he was out the door, she wasted no time hurrying over to Birch. Swede watched as she slipped the knife to him.

"Don't let them know you're free until they sit down to eat. Their guns will be set down then, and you'll have a better chance of escape."

"Why are you doing this?" Birch asked. Swede wondered the same thing. He had noticed that his partner had been working on his ropes all morning and they were loosening up. The two men might not be free before the Shirleys left, but after finding out that the brothers weren't inclined to kill, Swede and Birch weren't in any danger. Maybe Lulu was trying to get the two of them killed. He had the feeling that the Shirleys wouldn't mind shooting them if they tried to escape. Vardis Shirley could probably justify his action as self-defense.

"I don't want to go with them," she whispered, glancing at the door. "I'd rather take my chances with you."

Lulu straightened up and went back to the stove, where she started dishing up the meal just as the door opened. All four brothers marched in and sat down while Lulu served them. Clyde looked up at her and started to ask, "Uh, do you have—" but she interrupted him.

"Here's your meal, Clyde." She set a heaping plate down in front of him. As soon as he looked down at it, all thoughts of the knife were forgotten.

As she set Fergis's plate down, Lulu said in a stern tone, "Now, Fergis, you set that shotgun down properlike. I won't have any of you boys eating with your guns setting across your laps. Look at Vardis. He's laid his shotgun down on the floor."

She looked over at Birch meaningfully. Vardis's gun was the closest one to the prisoners, and even at that, it was still halfway across the room.

Out of the corner of his eye, Swede could see Birch sawing away at his ropes. In the meantime, Lulu took her full plate to the table and sat down with the brothers. But instead of eating, she began to entertain them with stories about some of the customers at the saloons. She soon had them laughing and hanging onto her every word.

Swede noticed that Birch wasn't sitting as stiffly in his chair as before. He glanced over and was relieved to see that Birch was surreptitiously rubbing his wrists to get some feeling back in them. A moment later, Birch had slipped out of his chair. Swede noted that the brothers were too busy shoveling food in their mouths and laughing at Lulu's stories to be aware that Birch was free. Everyone was turned away from Birch as he crept around in back of Vardis and grabbed a shotgun. "Don't anybody move. Keep your hands on the table," Birch ordered in a calm voice.

All four brothers stopped what they were doing. Clyde's food began falling out of his mouth; Homer was wide-eyed, still in mid-chew, one cheek puffed out like a squirrel storing nuts; Fergis had his fork poised, and when he saw Birch standing there, his expression darkened and he swore, "How the hell did he get loose?" Everyone turned to look at Lulu, who had been the only one to move. She had stood up and backed away from the table.

Birch had moved away from the table at an angle so he could see all the Shirleys. Vardis started to get up, turning his head toward Birch, as if he were going to speak. Birch raised the gun slightly and shook his head. Vardis sat back down.

"Kick all the guns away from the table," Birch ordered. "And Vardis here can slowly get out the key to the handcuffs and toss them toward me. Lulu, you come pick them up and free Swede."

"I don't think you're going to get away with this, son," Vardis said softly. "It'll take more than you two to take all of us in."

"We'll manage, Vardis," Birch said.

After Lulu freed Swede, he stood up and stretched.

"Whenever you want to start tying these men up, go ahead," Birch told Swede, without taking his eyes off the Shirleys.

"I'll just get some rope," Swede replied. He found the rope outside in one of the saddlebags. The horses were all ready for travel, and soon the Shirleys were tied up and ready for travel as well.

Birch and Swede mounted their horses. But as they gazed at their handiwork, Swede felt as if something was missing. Or someone. "Where's Lulu?" he asked suddenly, looking around.

Birch shrugged. "I guess she slipped away sometime after she freed you. We were both too busy getting these boys ready to deliver to the sheriff."

Swede frowned. He hated loose ends. "If you wait here, I can go after her," he offered. "She couldn't have gotten far on foot." He started to spur his horse, but Birch held up his hand.

"Let's just leave it, Swede. We've got to start out now if we want to reach town before dark," Birch said, an enigmatic look on his face.

Reluctantly, Swede agreed, and they set out, the Shirleys grumbling and whining the whole way to Grass Valley.

CHAPTER 23

"WELL, I'm impressed," Sheriff Martin said, stepping back to survey his handiwork. All four Shirleys sat dejectedly in his cells: Homer and Fergis in one cell, Clyde and Vardis in the other one. The sheriff turned to Birch and Swede and said, "We'd just about given up on you. Since we hadn't heard from you in a couple of days, I was going to wire your boss, Arthur Tisdale, today."

Birch replied, "You might not have heard from us for another day or two if we hadn't had a bit of luck. The Shirleys know the hills around here better than anybody, and that was their advantage. Until now."

"Let's go back into the office," the sheriff said, shepherding Birch and Swede toward the door. He turned back to the Shirleys and tipped his hat. "See you all later."

Back in the office, Deputy Jim Wells was sitting at a desk. When Birch and Swede came in, Wells looked at them with admiration. "Tell us the whole story," he said, eagerly leaning forward. "They looked pretty tough."

Sheriff Martin grinned at the deputy's enthusiasm and replied, "Well, they don't look so troublesome anymore."

Birch and Swede sat down and took turns telling their story. When Birch got to the part where he was taken prisoner as well, the deputy's eyes practically popped out of his head. "How did you get away?"

Chet Martin curled his lip at the young man, but good humor still twinkled in his eyes as he chided, "If you'd stop interrupting these men, they could get to the finish sooner."

Properly chastised, Jim Wells listened to the rest of the

tale without interrupting. When Birch and Swede finally fell silent, the deputy couldn't resist saying, "That's quite an adventure. I hope I can say I've done something like that someday. You not only caught the bank robbers, but one of them's a murderer."

Birch looked at Swede, then back at Martin and Wells. "That's something I left out, Sheriff," Birch said. "I don't think the Shirleys robbed that bank in Nevada City."

"Why do you think that?"

"They said they didn't."

Sheriff Martin looked skeptical. Even Deputy Wells was frowning.

"Now, Birch," the sheriff replied, "of course they wouldn't admit to robbing that bank. A bank clerk was killed. They might admit to the other robberies, but don't expect them to tell you the truth about a murder."

Birch smiled. "They didn't tell me anything. We overheard them talking while we were still trussed up. They had no reason to lie then. They thought they were going to get away."

The lawman seemed to turn this over in his mind before finally accepting this reasoning. "Marshal McManus is going to be awful disappointed if the killer isn't caught. He might try to hang it on one of the Shirleys anyway," Martin warned. "Do you think that bank was robbed by another gang?"

"No," Birch said, "but I have an idea who might have robbed the bank and killed Joe Child. Of course, I can't prove it, but I'm riding over to Nevada City tonight to have a little talk with my suspect."

The sheriff frowned. "Who is it?"

"Cyrus Dundee, the bank clerk."

Martin raised his eyebrows. "The eyewitness? Why?"

"For someone who was vague about the descriptions of the robbers, he sure picked the Shirleys out fast," Birch explained. "But there was more to it than that. It has to do with Miss Lulu Montana."

Martin nodded. "The saloon singer. She was the one who supplied information to the Shirleys."

"She was Emmet Shirley's widow, a brother who died on the way out to California four years ago," Birch began. "She would go to a town and pick a saloon to sing in, a likely looking saloon where stagecoach drivers might drink, or bank tellers. She never worked in Nevada City. At the time of that robbery, she was in Oroville, seventy-five miles away."

"With that information, plus the fact that the Shirleys are against killing anyone because of the consequences," Swede concluded, "Birch was able to figure out who the real killer was."

Wells interrupted. "Say, where is Lulu Montana? Why didn't you bring her in as well?"

Again, Swede and Birch exchanged a look. Swede finally answered. "She slipped away while we were busy tying up the Shirleys. By now, she's well away from here."

"Do you want us to put out a poster? Rhodes and Valentine might want to offer a reward."

"No, that's all right," Birch said a little too quickly. He amended with, "She helped us escape, so I feel we owe her that much."

"Besides," Swede added, "I don't think she poses much of a threat. Lulu was tied to the Shirley gang by marriage. I don't think she would have ever thought about bank robbery as a living if she hadn't married into the family."

The sheriff was silent for a minute, then nodded his head. "All right. I'll trust you. Why don't you stay here for the night? You can start out for Nevada City tomorrow morning with Deputy Wells."

Birch stood and shook his head. "Thanks for the offer, Sheriff, but we'd better get over there tonight."

★ ★ ★

When they rode into Nevada City, Birch was surprised to find Marshal McManus still in his office. McManus looked up when the ex-Texas Ranger and his partner entered.

"What can I do for you, Birch?" McManus leaned back in his chair and rubbed the bridge of his nose.

Birch introduced Swede. Then he took his hat off and said, "Marshal, we have the Shirley gang in jail back in Grass Valley."

McManus straightened up in his chair, his expression almost friendly. "Well, damn, that's great. I never thought anyone'd ever catch those brothers." The marshal stood up and came around his desk. He grabbed Birch's hand and shook it. "I don't normally do this, but I owe you an apology. I thought old Vern Rhodes was wasting his money on some fancy-pants investigator, but you sure proved your mettle. Which one of those sons-of-a-bitch did it?"

Birch blinked. "Did what?"

"Killed Joe Child. Which one?"

Birch rubbed his forehead and grimaced. "None of them killed him."

The marshal stared at him for a moment in disbelief. Finally, he said, "What are you trying to tell me?"

"Why don't you sit down and let me give you a short version of the story." Five minutes later, McManus was nodding, although still skeptical about the innocence of the Shirley gang.

"Tell me something, Marshal," Birch said. "Has Cyrus Dundee been acting strange these last few days? Has he talked about going on any trips?"

McManus shook his head. "Not that I know of." He stood up and gathered up his hat. "Why don't we take a walk over to Vern Rhodes's house and ask him. He sees Cyrus every day."

Rhodes came to the door wearing a nightshirt that strained at the seams to cover his belly. With grumpy reluctance, the banker received the trio. But he appeared to wake up when he was given news about the Shirleys.

"Well," he said expansively, "that was worth waking me up." Rhodes clapped the marshal on the back and grinned. "Who wants to celebrate with me? Brandy, anyone?" He moved over to the liquor cabinet and started to pour himself a stiff drink. "Marshal?" McManus shook his head and politely declined. Birch and Swede followed suit.

"Tell me, Mr. Rhodes," Birch replied, "has Cyrus Dundee done anything unusual lately?"

Rhodes scratched his ample stomach. "Not that I can think of. But do you know what he did the other day? He up and quit. Today was his last day. Said he's got an offer from a bank in San Francisco." Rhodes grunted. "It'll be damned hard to replace him as well as Child."

Birch pulled the marshal aside. "Will you stay here and explain it to him while Swede and I go talk to Dundee? Then come join us as soon as you're done."

McManus grumbled about being left behind, but he was a good lawman and knew that this was the most efficient way to handle the problem.

Birch and Swede walked over to Cyrus Dundee's little house. When the former clerk came to the door, he was surprised to see Birch.

"Mr. Birch! Please come in. And introduce me to your friend." He stepped aside to let the two men into his neatly kept parlor. "To what do I owe this pleasure? Have you captured the Shirley gang?"

"Yes, we have," Birch said, watching for any sign of fear or anxiety in Dundee. "They're in the Grass Valley jail at the moment. We'd like you to come identify them for us tomorrow."

"Oh," Dundee began, hesitating, "well, I see no reason why not. If you don't know already, I suppose I should tell you. I'm leaving Nevada City for San Francisco and had planned on taking tomorrow's stagecoach, but I suppose I could wire the bank and leave the day after. Can you come back tomorrow morning and I'll accompany you to Grass Valley?"

Although Birch was surprised by Dundee's openness, he had the feeling that Dundee wouldn't be here tomorrow when they came to pick him up. Birch thought quickly. "That would be fine, but could you please answer some questions? Swede will ask them while I get a glass of water." Before Dundee could reply, Birch walked out of the room toward what he assumed was the kitchen. He could hear Swede asking questions and Dundee answering them in an impatient tone.

In the hallway, he saw a partially shut door. Instinctively, he pushed it open to reveal a dingy bedroom. There was a bed with a shabby bedspread and a small table that served as a nightstand. A washstand stood in one corner and a highboy in the opposite corner. A bulging carpetbag sat in a chair near the washstand.

Birch picked up the bag, put it on the bed, and emptied it one item at a time. The bag held only the rudiments of traveling—two neatly folded and rolled-up shirts, one extra pair of pants, a vest, several collars and cuffs, and two ties. At first, Birch was disappointed. He had been wrong. He had reached the bottom of the carpetbag and there was no money. Maybe Dundee had hidden it somewhere else.

He started to look around, but his instinct told him to inspect the bag more closely. He finally found a discrepancy between the bottom inside the bag and the bottom on the outside. He pried the inside bottom away and found what he was looking for: neatly stacked paper worth approximately one thousand three hundred dollars.

As he walked back to the living room, he heard Cyrus Dundee's raised voice. "But that's ridiculous. Of course the Shirley gang robbed the bank and killed Joe. Who else would do such a thing?" His voice held a hint of nervousness as he added, "By the way, Mr. Birch has been in the kitchen an awfully long time. I'd better go find out if he's gotten his water."

Cyrus Dundee turned toward the kitchen just as Birch came in the front room, holding the carpetbag in front of him. Dundee froze, his eyes widening behind his thick bifocals, his shoulders slumping inward.

Marshal McManus knocked on the door, and Swede let him in.

"I thought I could get away with it," Dundee said numbly as the marshal handcuffed him. "All that money coming in regularly, it was hard to resist."

"Why did you kill Joe?" Birch asked.

"I didn't mean to," Dundee said miserably, "but he came back early."

The marshal frowned. "But you told me that you had just come back from lunch. Where had Joe gone?"

"Joe liked a beer in the afternoon. Mr. Rhodes didn't approve of drinking on the job, so I told Joe that he had enough time to slip over to the nearest saloon before Rhodes came back from his meal."

"But Joe came back early," Swede prompted.

"Yes," Dundee replied. He was shaking as he recounted that day. "I planned to shoot the gun and when people came running, I'd say the bank had been robbed. But he caught me and asked me what I was doing. I panicked and shot him."

With that, Dundee collapsed.

"I'd better get him over to the jail," McManus said. "You two want to come along?"

"I think it's time for us to ride back to Grass Valley," Birch said. "Swede has a stagecoach to catch tomorrow afternoon."

The marshal thanked them once again before escorting his prisoner, and the money, out the door.

CHAPTER 24

THE two friends had one last drink together before Swede left on the noon stagecoach to Sacramento. As soon as the telegraph office opened that morning, he had wired his wife that he would be home in a few days, right after they had met with the sheriff and the owner of the Grass Valley Bank. Harold Valentine was very pleased that the bank robbers had been caught, and he was very impressed that Cyrus Dundee was in custody as well.

"You've done quite a job," Valentine said, shaking their hands. "I'll be sending a bonus to you through Mr. Tisdale."

The sheriff rubbed his chin in thought. "What I don't understand is why Cyrus Dundee didn't flee long before this. He could have left Nevada City any time after the robbery and murder."

Swede shook his head and said, "He was too smart. Dundee knew that suspicion would fall on him if he left town right after the robbery. He planned on staying there for at least a few weeks."

"As it turned out," Birch added, "we put all the pieces together just in time. He was planning to leave on the stagecoach today."

Birch and Swede shook hands with, and again accepted thanks from, both Valentine and Sheriff Martin before taking their leave.

"I wish there was a way of getting word to Lulu that she isn't a wanted outlaw," Birch said as they headed for the stagecoach stop. .

"She'll eventually figure it out. She deserves a second

chance," Swede replied. "I honestly don't think she would have gotten involved in robbery if she hadn't married into the Shirley family."

The stagecoach had arrived. The two men stood just outside, waiting for the driver to finish loading the stagecoach with baggage.

Swede squinted against the bright, white-hot sun. "Why don't you try to find her? Maybe it would work out—"

"No," Birch said shortly. "It's better this way."

Swede studied his friend for a moment, then let out a short bark of laughter. "You can be a hard man sometimes, Birch. You don't bend. Someday, you might break."

Birch grinned. "I'll take that chance, Swede. Give my best to Greta." He looked down as he said it so that Swede wouldn't see his expression.

"You will come up to Grant's Pass soon, won't you? Greta has heard me talk so much about you that she wants to meet you."

"Yes. Someday."

"You're always welcome up there," Swede said solemnly.

They shook hands. Swede helped an elderly lady into the stagecoach, then climbed in after her.

The driver shouted out, "Anyone for Sacramento, the stage is leaving now."

Another passenger, a sweaty, pudgy little man just barely made it in time, carelessly flinging his bag onto the stagecoach roof before climbing in. Birch watched the stagecoach pull out and head west. When Swede stuck his arm out the window and waved, Birch raised his arm in a final farewell until all he could see was clouds of dust.

Some months later, Birch rode into a small town late at night. He was on the trail of a killer and was looking for a place to sleep for a few hours. He was thirsty from the dusty trail, and the bright lights of a small saloon loomed up in front of him. As he reined Cactus in at the hitching post, he heard a familiar voice inside the saloon, sweetly singing "Beautiful Dreamer."

He hesitated only a moment, then turned Cactus back in the direction he had been traveling and kept on riding through the night.